THE LONG

WINDING

ROAD

JANE R. CARVER

THE LONG WINDING ROAD
Copyright © 2023 by Jane R. Carver

ISBN: 979-8-88653-213-5

Published by Satin Romance
An Imprint of Melange Books, LLC
White Bear Lake, MN 55110
www.satinromance.com

Published in the United States of America.

Cover Design by Ashley Redbird Designs

The Beatles sang me through college. Their song, <u>The Long and Winding Road</u>, started the idea for this novel.

For Sue and Howie who told us all about Australia before we went there. They added more inspiration.

And Russell Crowe and the Man from Snowy River might have added a bit of flavor, too.

Thank you to my editor, Linda Mahoney Johnson, for helping make a great story for you.

An even bigger thank you to Miss Nancy at Melange. I think the world of you and respect what you've made of Melange-books. Some day we might even meet.

Chapter One

Together

"I'll be fine." Sarah patted Sharon Bannerman's arm in an attempt to reassure the older woman. "It's a corner pub. The concierge assured us this place would be fine for a small meal and drink. He says the North Union Bull is a quiet corner for a pint."

"I don't know, dear." Sharon cut her eyes to Harvey, her husband of fifty years. "You're so quiet, Harvey. What do you think, dear?"

"I thought I'd wait until you asked for my opinion. Then you'd listen. If I butt in, you'd ignore me." He sent a grin Sarah's way. "That's how it's gone for years. I finally learned to be patient."

"So? Will Sarah be safe in a corner pub alone until we get there?" Sharon picked up her purse and light sweater even as she asked.

"We're only visiting for an hour, Sharon. Not spending the day. Sarah's a big girl and can take care of herself. I mean, the concierge vouched for this place. What can happen?"

———

Sarah entered the North Union Bull pub with only a bit of trepidation. So far, their travel party, which included her, Sharon and Harvey Bannerman and Cary and Ann Switzer found Australia and Darwin, in particular, a delight. Sharon and Harvey were especially generous, friends of her parents. They invited her along on her semester break and paid for most of the trip, much to her dismay.

"A teaching salary doesn't allow for great adventures, sweetheart," Harvey told her when she tried to protest. "We've been to Australia several times and would love to show you places we enjoy. Now we'll hear nothing else about it."

So Sarah gave in graciously.

This particular day started out with a bit of chill, this country being south of the equator, nearing winter while at home in New Jersey, summer lay ahead. She had two weeks to explore the world of a man she admired and yearned to know personally. *Never going to happen,* she often reminded herself, but she never gave up that dream.

The interior of the corner pub featured a bar so like the ones she saw on the BBC mystery TV shows that she felt at home almost immediately. A wide corner broke up the bar top so people leaning against the wood could talk friendly-like to those at the other side.

"What can I get you, love?" A burly man stood behind the bar, its top so shiny that sunlight through the window created a glare off the polished wood. The man stood almost at attention behind the burnished bar, a spotless towel draped over one arm, with a satin vest layered over a crisp white shirt, sleeves rolled up to the elbows.

Sarah couldn't catch her grin in time, and the man saw, didn't frown exactly but did ask, "Problem, love?"

"I hope I haven't offended you, but I expected an over-weight man with a spotty apron tied around his middle to be handing out the drinks. You exceed my expectations, sir."

Seeing that Sarah wasn't mocking him or worse, criticizing him, the man waved her forward to the bar and nodded in a friendly way. "You're from the States, I hear. Not the south part either, I'm thinking. What can I get you then?"

"Something local, I think. I can get all kinds of beers where I live on the east coast, but I want what the guys here drink. I'll never make it to your country again, so I want some great memories to take home with me."

"Right you are. One Toohey's Old Dark Ale coming up. On the draft as it should be." He turned to taps lined up behind him, pulled over two glasses but turned back to Sarah before pulling the handle. "A pint?" He held up a small brandy snifter-sized glass. "Or a pony?" This glass looked more like a typical draft beer glass.

Tempted as she was to have a pint, she was alone and would be for a bit, so she opted for the smaller brew. "Pony please. At least for starters." She gave him a grin that promised to buy a second brew if this one suited her.

"One coldie right here. Sip this, and you may recognize a bit of chocolate and coffee with a slight hint of caramel." He slid the glass in front of Sarah and braced his hands against the bar, apparently waiting on her opinion.

One sip and she gave a delicate cough which set the bar man to grinning.

"It's a bit stronger than I'm used to, but that taste is amaz-ing." She took another sip but held this one on her tongue.

Her taste buds analyzed the beer. After a slow swallow, she nodded and lifted the glass in respect. "Oh yeah, I caught the chocolate. Haven't found the caramel yet but I think the coffee flavor hit the back of my tongue when I swallowed."

"That's a heap of good, miss." The man fairly beamed. He gave her a satisfied jerk of a nod then headed to the other end of the bar where another customer called for him.

With the time somewhere between breakfast and lunch, Sarah knew better than to take more than sips and stretched the drink out. The bar man would plunk another in front of her as soon as she emptied this glass. Two of this dark ale and she might not be steady for lunch with Sharon and Harvey.

Thinking of that, she turned her back to the bar, drink in hand, and surveyed the small pub's interior. Not more than three feet away were tables where four could sit for lunch. The tables were heavy affairs with wide legs and claw feet. Booths lined the walls along the window sides of the pub. The ceiling was lower than she expected, used to more spacious bars with tall ceilings in the states.

"Even a university prof gets to bars once in a while," she muttered as she took another sip. Glancing down, she noted the glass was now half-empty. Her head still straight and her vision un-blurred, she figured she was good for another ten minutes or so before she reached the bottom of this pony.

She turned back to the bar, propped her elbows on the top and soaked up the atmosphere, imagining she could see her favorite BBC TV detectives having a pint along the other side. The door opened and closed a number of times. A few of the newcomers came to the bar for drinks then disappeared behind her at tables or booths. Satisfied with the world at the moment, she raised her pony of dark ale to the absent Sharon Bannerman. "I'm just fine."

The words barely left her mouth before all hell broke loose behind her.

Two men standing toe to toe between the door and herself drew her attention. Voices rose, and cursing broke out.

"You sorry wanker! That's my woman you made eyes at last night!"

"Bugger off. Your old woman's a slagger."

That did it! Suddenly her quiet little corner bar exploded into a full-scale fistfight. Chairs fell over, and a table skidded to one side. Dang, this was beginning to look just like a movie. Only problem was it was for real. And she had never seen men throw real punches and try to injure each other before.

The fight moved in her direction. Fists swinging and blows drawing groans, this was shaping up to be a major drama, and she wanted no part of it.

She leaned in closer to the bar, clutching her drink. Two men with a disagreement in this *safe* pub were turning the place into a boxing arena from the sounds of it.

Afraid to move, with no help coming from the bar man who was on the phone at the moment, no doubt calling the police, Sarah huddled near the corner of the bar, hoping the fight was short-lived and far from her. To be honest, though, no bigger than this pub was, the fight was probably within ten feet of her.

Finding an exit was uppermost in her mind. The two fighters were moving toward her fast. It was scaring the crap out of her especially when they pushed into her and slammed her into a man who grabbed her to keep her from going down in the middle of the intense situation.

He drew her body out of the way but kept his arms around her so she wouldn't fall, and he could pull her further away if needed. She wrapped her arms around him so tight, she figured she'd probably cut off his air, but just watching those guys punch and roll scared her.She buried her face into his neck as the two men fought on. She tried to crawl into the man's skin she was that frightened!

At one point, one of the two men fighting picked up a piece of chair leg and threw it at the other man. But it bounced off the other assailant's shoulder and flew straight at the pair at the bar. The protector pulled her even closer if that was possible and turned his back to the flying object. It struck him on the shoulder, but by then the object had lost a lot of momentum. Her left arm hugged the man's ribs as her right arm clamped tightly onto his upper arm. The muscles there bunched and rippled as he maneuvered her against the bar with his back to the chaos that was erupting into a major ordeal.

"Stand still. I'll catch the brunt of..." Ooof! Whoever stood between her and the men brawling must have caught a punch or else been shoved. Shoved, definitely, because the taller body protecting Sarah grunted and pushed into her backside.

"Are you all right?" she managed to ask though she wasn't sure the man heard her.

The sound of shrill police whistles coming through the door drowned out his reply if he even made one. Within minutes, the police arrived and started breaking up the fight. Eventually they hauled off the two fighters.

"Good on you, Constable Young. Many thanks, mate," called the bar man. "One free round on the house, mates." He started setting up a round of drinks while a young man who worked there righted the furniture and tossed the odd broken chair leg behind the bar.

Though the comparative quiet was deafening, Sarah trembled with fright. She still had her head buried in the man's neck. She didn't want to see the fight so hadn't even looked up at him yet. The man talked quietly to her, trying to help her calm down.

"You all right, miss? I worried I'd not get to you in time or perhaps hurt you when those two backed up into me."

His voice was deep and rumbled through his chest. She pulled her face out of his neck and laid it on his shoulder as she looked around. The chills that passed through her as the violence rolled around them began to subside. The man who held her so closely spoke tenderly and very low, speaking nonsense that she really wasn't paying attention to, but heard. The sound of his voice was soothing.

At some point, she started listening to the man who still held her wrapped to him. And then she stiffened. It finally got through to her panic-filled brain that she *knew* that voice. He must have felt the change because he loosened his grip on her but remained with his arms around her. She still had not looked at him, but now she pulled her head back and slowly allowed her eyes to travel from his chest up the neck that really needed a shave to a chin that had dark stubble on it to eyes of forest green. There he was...the man she had loved for so long. Everything suddenly blurred and slowed as if the whole incident had been a dream leading her up to this precise moment in time.

All she could do was stare at him; perhaps her mouth fell open just a bit. He looked down at Sarah with a smile on those gorgeous lips. When she said nothing, his smile slowly disappeared. A small frown pulled the lines of his forehead together. He didn't understand her reaction to him.

Where's all the air? I can't breathe! Sarah tried sucking in much needed air to speak...say anything. To thank this man she knew so well yet didn't. What a contradiction. How would she even be able to breathe again after being in his arms? How would she ever live after stepping out of his arms?

Thankfully, a voice calling her from across the bar spared her attempt to make sense of her confused thinking. That sound broke the trance she had fallen in to.

"Sarah? Sweetheart, are you okay?" Sharon made her way

through the remaining mess to stand next to the couple. Harvey followed close behind. "Dear, what happened?"

"An old-fashioned barroom fight, Sharon." If Sarah's smile sat a bit crooked on her face and her light laughter seemed a bit strained, that should have explained her pale face. "That's what happened. But I'm all right. Really." She added that because Sharon looked skeptical, her brows raised, one brow cocked up, her own complexion going a shade lighter.

"Are you sure, dear?" Sharon stepped up to Sarah and put her arms around her before pulling back to give her face a good long examination.

"Absolutely. I had protection."

Sharon spoke just as Sarah said *protection,* so the older woman missed that intriguing comment.

"Harvey and I were just coming to find you and tell you we met some friends from the States who invited us up for the weekend, but we don't want to leave you alone if something like this is going to happen." Sharon wrung her hands together, as her eyes shot left then right, checking that no one lay bloodied on the floor. "Normally us going in different directions isn't a problem. Now I'm not sure we should go. You really need protection, my dear."

"I'll take care of her." The deep voice came from Sarah's side. She forgot that her guardian still held her in an embrace against his side. Did he just offer to stay with her while the Bannermans visited friends? She wasn't sure which emotion held her hardest: the thrill of the offer to spend a weekend with a man she'd admired for years—and maybe had a crush on—or the shock of his offer. While she knew all about this man, at least professionally, he knew nothing about her, professionally or otherwise.

Though Sharon might not have noticed the handsome man who held Sarah, Harvey had. "Sir, it seems you took care of Sarah while a tornado tore this bar apart," he laughed, "but we don't even know you."

At that, Sarah came out of her daze and shook her head, knowing *she* could make introductions. Explanations to this man would have to wait until formalities were taken care of.

"I'm sorry. Sharon and Harvey Bannerman, this is Reagan Conley. Reagan, Sharon, Harvey and I, as well as another couple, are traveling together through this part of Australia. When we want to go our separate ways, we just let each other know and head off." Sarah smiled at the older couple but was afraid to look up at Reagan.

She could tell by the way he clutched her waist when she spoke that he was full of questions. How in the world did she know him? That had to be what he was thinking. It was so blatantly obvious to her that it was a wonder the Bannermans didn't ask him what was wrong. Of course, they knew some things that he didn't...like Sarah's lifelong love of his photography. Maybe they weren't quite as aware of her love of him as a man, though she suspected Harvey knew.

Reagan Conley let go of Sarah long enough to shake Harvey's hand and again offered to look after her over the weekend while they visited up country. With what appeared to be easy acceptance, the husband and wife thanked him. They each kissed Sarah on the cheek, told her they'd see her Monday morning and then they made their way out of the bar...all within five minutes of that earth-shattering fist fight.

So there they stood...still locked in an embrace. Sarah felt foolish, embarrassed. She owed him an explanation. But it really was impossible to think when the smell of warm skin, mild cologne and *man* floated around her. What a heady combination of aromas.

"You want to tell me what that was all about?" Reagan asked with a laugh in his voice. If Sarah lived to be a hundred, she would always be thankful that he didn't get mad at her for what she had just put him through. It only made her love him more if that was possible.

"I owe you a big explanation, don't I?" she asked as she examined his chest closely. She had trouble meeting his eyes.

Still holding her to his chest, Reagan leaned an elbow on the bar and, tucking his captive closer into one arm, he lifted her chin so she would finally meet his gaze. He tilted his head to one side, crocked a tiny smile at her, and waited.

The few photographs Sarah had of him and the short video of him narrating a lecture didn't do Reagan Conley justice at all. Rich dark hair fell over his forehead and curled slightly behind his neck. Dark eyebrows arched up as he watched her watching him. Tiny crow's feet arrowed out from the corners of his eyes, eyes that were the color of a forest... deep green. A straight nose broke the line of high cheekbones. His mouth was almost too small but curved into such a sweet line that one could be forgiven that last thought. A faint shadow indicated the tiny cleft in his chin. His shoulders were broad and well-muscled, as was the arm she still clutched. As her fingers spread out along the curve of his ribs, she could tell there was no fat on this man. He lived lean and hard. It was the nature of his job. They fit together so well...his body and hers.

Lord please, can I always stay this way? But that's not possible. The time has come to explain.

So Sarah began.

"My name is Sarah Malloy. I'm a teaching doctor at Princeton University in New Jersey back in the States. I teach creative writing, and I use your photographs along with music and some films to motivate students to not only write but to exceed their own expectations. I've got every picture you've ever taken, I think. At least every one that's been published." She spoke slowly, for to speak fast would rob her of the air she needed to talk and admire this man at the same time. He was so perfect.

"It seems you know all about me," he commented as he nodded to the bartender, indicating they would both have a beer.

"I know all about the photographs, but little about the man." She could have kicked herself as soon as the words left her mouth, but it was too late. That was a pretty telling statement and almost sounded like an invitation. But he didn't seem to take offense. If the man heard an invitation in her soft words, he didn't indicate it.

"Another set up, mate?" he called to the bar man.

"Coming up." The same man wearing that same satin vest who calmly called the police while a fight raged in his establishment placed a pint beside Reagan and another pony glass in front of her.

"Ta, mate," Reagan told the man.

He turned Sarah toward the bar, while he stood just behind her. Moving the pony of Toohey's to her hand, he grabbed his pint, lifted the brew and offered a salute.

"Here's to knowing more about the man." He waited for her to say something before he drank. Glancing over her shoulder at his face, she saw that he was once more smiling and relaxed. Raising her own glass, Sarah agreed with him.

"To the man," she said and took a deep drink. Never had Sarah uttered such enticing words with so much promise just waiting to be claimed. She drank a good third of the beer as her heart raced.

What would the next few days offer? Hell, what would the next few minutes offer? He could laugh at her, thank her for admiring his work then walk out of her life as quickly as he had entered it. That thought alone terrified her. Him leaving? Never to see him? Never to touch him again?

Actually, it turned out to be quite easy. Sarah remained

standing belly up to the bar while he leaned around her and again rested that elbow on the polished wood. "Still shaky after that dust up?" He sipped his beer while waiting for her to answer.

"I've never seen a real fist fight. Anyone that dares to say it's exciting would be lying." She twisted the glass round and round but only met his eyes on the word *lying*.

"I've seen more fights in places like this all over the world than you have time to listen to."

His relaxed stance and knowing smile coupled with a faraway gaze drew Sarah's attention.

"Who says I don't have time to listen to those stories?" She sounded a little wicked perhaps, but her tiny smile kept the question from being too forward.

"Good thing this place is on the outskirts of Darwin. I have a small bungalow on the beach about forty minutes from here. No tourists will bother us there. Come spend the afternoon with me, and we'll talk of bar fights and schoolrooms." Reagan still leaned against the bar, but the anticipation on his face belied his casual stance.

He's serious! Sarah's heart sped up again. A blush rose to her cheeks. A tiny tremble went through her again. He wants to spend time with me. How can I refuse? I can't. No way.

"I'd like that very much, Reagan," was her soft reply. She held her breath to see what he'd do when she agreed to his proposal.

He didn't disappoint. He grinned so wide that she thought his face would split.

"Fantastic! Come on, then, finish the glass, and let's go find that sand. Daylight's wasting." Throwing his head back, he knocked off the rest of his beer as if it were water. Barely allowing her time to swallow the last of her own drink, Reagan grabbed Sarah's hand and swung her toward the door.

She couldn't help the laugh that escaped. He's so enthusiastic about an idea of spending an afternoon with me. Elation flooded her nerves, and she wanted to dance through the door.

"Daylight's wasting'...really! It's only one o'clock on Friday afternoon," she called to him as he hustled her down the cobbled sidewalk.

This is the beginning of a perfect weekend, she prayed.

Chapter Two

They made their way down the busy boulevard, passed the last of businesses, into the country. Almost to forty minutes on the dot, Reagan turned off the main road and followed the winding tarmac until he stopped in front of a small house.

"Don't let the looks fool you. It's great inside." He bounced out of the car and rounded to her side.

Sarah agreed that the weather-beaten exterior lacked what those in the States would call *curb appeal*, but she couldn't wait to see if the interior lived up to Reagan's promise. After all, he was a professional photojournalist with an eye for beauty, so she trusted his judgment.

"Oh, Reagan." She breathed the words out slowly. She was right to trust him. The interior was subdued in seaside colors of pale blue, gold, tan and coral. Artful but spacious without the usual rental clutter. Sarah loved it at first sight.

"Come see this view." Reagan called for her to follow him as he made his way through the front room and headed to a set of double doors. Throwing them open, he stood aside and, with a sweep of his arm, urged her to step on to the terrace. "What do you think of that?"

Coming from the dim light of the house into the full brightness of the afternoon, Sarah was momentarily blinded. As her eyes adjusted, she held her breath yet again.

"Your patch of beach is impressive, Reagan." She went to the rail and leaned forward to scan first one way then the other. White sand covered the landscape from under the edge of the deck out across the expanse to drown in the surf that was coming in. The only sound was the lap of pale gray waves as they rolled back out to the ocean. Beyond the immediate pale gray near the shore, the water took on a crisp bluish tint that stretched to the horizon.

A few gulls dipped and rose above the shallow waves near the beach.

"Is that a sea gull?" Sarah pointed to a group standing on the sand, a few occasionally flying up but returning to the sand.

"Silver gulls. Oh look, an albatross!" Reagan leaned into her side and pointed so she could follow his finger.

"Oh, Reagan, it's lovely." Sarah whispered. She threw a quick glance at him but turned to the sight of the beach again. "Can we go out soon?"

"Kick off your shoes and socks, find something to wear for swimming, and I'll do the same. Then we'll grab a beach 'brella, some food and a camera and off we go." He suited action to words as he darted around gathering things he felt they needed. As he left the deck to check the kitchen for food and drinks, Sarah pondered what to wear. She didn't have a swimsuit on, but her panties and bra were dark and matched. It wasn't exactly what polite society might wear, but it would do. If she could just talk Reagan out of a T-shirt to wear, then she might not get sunburn.

"Reagan, do you have a T shirt I can borrow so I won't

burn?"

"Look in my bedroom. The housekeeper did the wash and left them folded in there." She followed his directions and pulled out a white shirt that sported some East Indian logo she didn't recognize.

Checking on Reagan's whereabouts, she quickly pulled off her polo shirt and pulled Reagan's larger shirt over her head. Unzipping and removing her jeans, she looked at her image in the full-length mirror in the washroom.

"Well, modesty is served," she conceded with a laugh. Reagan's shirt hit her at the kneecaps! Rolling the sleeves up at her shoulders, she went through the house until she found him in the other room, kneeling before a case. A cooler lay on the floor nearby along with towels and suntan lotion.

"What's that?" Sarah asked as she knelt beside Reagan. She could see what looked like some kind of equipment, but the man's hands were in the way so she couldn't tell for sure exactly what was in the case.

"Oh, this? I never travel *anywhere* without a camera! You never know when a photograph will beg to be taken. Some of my best pictures have been spur of the moment shots that I would have missed if I hadn't had a camera right there."

Though the man was in his late thirties like her, he looked so much like a little boy at that moment, she reached over and hugged him. She drew back immediately, but not before she could tell he enjoyed the brief touch. His grin and softening expression of his eyes gave him away.

"Come on, help me put this stuff by the back door." Together they carried everything outside.

Reagan walked over to another set of double doors that opened on to the deck and opened them. "Back in a tick."

The doors led to his bedroom where Sarah could see her street clothes laid out on his bed. She decided to wait on the deck for him, but saw when he picked up her shirt, put it to his nose and inhaled. It reminded her so much of how she had acted in the bar that she sighed. How she literally buried her nose in his shirt as he protected her from the fighters. If only he could feel about her like she felt about him.

Sarah had come to love this man over years of time. Some would call her feelings a crush. He saw with his camera what spoke to her heart. That same heart ached with the thought of him possibly loving her. Even as she gazed onto a sea that rushed in and rolled back, she shook her head. Better not to get her hopes up. Better to take this weekend and whatever came of it and accept the fact that she was flying back to New Jersey Tuesday morning, and she'd never see him again. Her eyes misted over just a little with that thought.

She didn't hear Reagan come back outside. Didn't know he was anywhere around until he stopped next to her and leaned over to look her in the face. Taking his hand and wiping it under her eye, he gave her a puzzled frown.

"Tears, Sarah, on a beautiful afternoon like this? What's wrong? Tell me. I'll fix it. Remember, I promised to keep you safe this weekend." As he talked, he kept that large warm hand wrapped around her cheek. "Tell me. Please."

"It's just the bright sun, Reagan. Nothing could possibly be *wrong*! Come on," she added. "Daylight's wasting! I think I heard someone say that not too long ago." She giggled and made a swipe at him when he reached over and tickled her.

"Come on then, woman...let's go find a comfy spot, frolic like dolphins, eat until we're stuffed, take a nice nap and talk about everything!" Grabbing her hands, he started piling things in her arms until she couldn't hold anything else. Pulling a very large beach umbrella out from behind some chairs, he carried that plus the camera bag and towels while Sarah carried the cooler, lotion and a pillow. The first step on to the sand had them hopping, it was so hot. But after a few seconds of jumping around, they grew used to it and plunged on across the sand in search of a place to settle for the afternoon.

Down the beach they strode, talking the entire time. They finally settled into one spot, set up the 'brella and scattered the rest of the goods about. Sarah spread a large blanket for them to use while Reagan arranged the pillow to his liking, ready for them to use later. But they were eager to test the waters before settling down to eat, rest and talk more. Reagan pulled her down to sit beside him. He had let her do her thing while he rubbed lotion on his legs and arms. Now he handed her the bottle.

"Put some on my back?" He turned his back to her and sat crossed legged.

Sarah accepted the bottle and watched Reagan's hands grip his knees a bit more tightly than she expected. Perhaps he was as nervous as her? Once again, her heart made a tripping motion in her breast. Oh God, to be able to touch him again... it was her fondest wish. That wish was coming true. Pouring some of the creamy liquid into her palm, she rubbed it between her hands and reached out to him. She almost stopped but after a second of hesitation, she laid both hands gently on his shoulders. His skin was warm and firm to the touch.

He jumped just a bit when she started moving her hands across his shoulders and down his back. He caught his breath for a second.

"That feels wonderful, love."

She knew too much about the way Australians spoke to take the word *love* as anything more personal than the word *mate*. She gloried in the feel of the lotion over his skin. He rolled his head as she soothed the lotion into the curve of his neck.

Would he ever want me like I do him, she wondered.

"Can I say something, Sarah, without you getting pissed

off?"

"Pissed off?"

"Angry. Annoyed."

"Oh, yes, go ahead. I doubt there's anything you could say to me that would make me angry." She continued to rub lotion across his shoulders as he relaxed into her hands.

"It's just this. I've known you for only a few hours on a Friday afternoon, and we have the whole weekend ahead of us. Together. And I..." He paused and bent his head around so he could see her. "You seem a quiet type, gentle ways. Soothing. Pleasing." He snapped his head around and slapped his knee. "Crikey. I sound like my gran."

"Reagan, just say what you want to, no matter how it comes out." The temperature wasn't making Sarah sweat. It was this hesitation to speak on Reagan's part that worried her, set her heart racing, slowed her hands.

"The longer I'm around you, the more I want to be around you. Does that make sense? You have a very calming effect on me, and that's something I can't remember experiencing in all this wanderlust I subject myself to." He spoke softly but quickly, as if the words needed out but fear held them back. "I want so many things in life, maybe you're one of those things. But..." he paused and gave her another long gaze, "I want to know you more. Better. You might be part of what I'm looking for...have been for a long time. I'm not even sure what that is, but I think you may have something to do with finding what I've been searching for."

Breathing was so hard. Sarah tried several times to pull in air, but her heart just took up all that room. He found her attractive? Calming? She'd take it! All of it and more. As long as he wasn't a mass murderer or a violent abuser, she'd be happy to help him find his way to an elusive goal...no matter what. Their time together would end far too soon, but the memories...oh the memories would last a lifetime.

What might have been an awkward silence turned out to be just that...a soft silence that neither bothered to break. The surf rolled. Birds squawked. Branches rustled along the verdant edge of forest.

Sarah sat behind Reagan, her hands resting on her thighs while he sat so near her she only had to lean forward a tiny bit and her breasts would touch his back. Time. We have time, she told herself.

Not sure how to answer Reagan's admission, she simply put her hand on his shoulder. "Not pissed...at all. Shall we see where the weekend leads?" A promise of sorts...as close as Sarah wanted to come to giving her heart openly to this man.

"Ta for the rub." Reagan nodded. "And the weekend. Ready for some of this on your delicate skin? New Jersey hasn't prepared you for Australian sun. Sit down and give me the lotion." Reagan acted very nonchalant, but anticipation filled his grin.

She turned her back to him and sat Indian style. Putting a hand over her shoulder, she asked, "Give me some lotion, and I'll put it on my legs while you're doing my back."

"No, let me take care of this first, and then we'll do the rest." He cleared his throat after that and waited for her to look back at him. When she did, he plucked a shoulder of the over-sized T-shirt she still wore. "This suntan lotion might go on easier if you took the shirt off first." He gave her a grin but let his gaze drift off to the trees.

Sweet man. He doesn't want me to feel self-conscious about disrobing in front of him.

Sarah smiled back, ducked her head, and pulled off the shirt then waited. Her underwear was beautiful in black satin and lace. Thankfully, it was full coverage and not one of the few skimpy pieces of lingerie she owned. Behind her, she heard Reagan suck in his breath, but she remained quiet, although a tiny secret smile of satisfaction touched her lips for a second.

If either spoke, it might break the spell. Sarah sat very straight while she listened for Reagan's movements. He poured lotion into his hands and laid his hand in the middle of her back. Like him, she drew in her breath, whether from the cool lotion or his touch, he would never know. Moving over her much smaller back, he made his motions small and gentle. Rising to her shoulders and near the straps of the lace bra, he worked but waited to see if she would move the straps or let him. Would he have to push the issue, or would she concede him the right to touch her intimately?

Slowly Sarah crossed her arms and raised them to the straps. Arching her back, she slipped the black band from each shoulder but kept the cups bound around her breasts. It cost her though. She was almost ready to give herself to Reagan Conley. Her nipples hardened, and her private parts throbbed. Her vagina grew wet. If Reagan had turned her to him that moment and taken her, he would have found her ready...body and soul. But he continued to rub in the lotion.

Maybe it's too soon for him, she thought.

He finished his ministrations along her upper and lower back and ribs then slowly pulled the straps back up. But before he lay the fabric back, he placed a soft kiss on each shoulder. Then as if nothing had happened, he came around in front of her, took hold of her hand and squeezed lotion into it.

"Rub this on your arms while I get your legs." He looked into her eyes when she didn't move. "Get a move on," he told her, then he whispered to her in an undertone, "We'll get back to this other thing later."

Oh, what a promise! She'd hold him to that. If he could wait, then so could she. Sarah had no idea if Reagan knew how much this waiting cost her, but she suspected it cost him just as much in patience as her.

So saying, he began rubbing the liquid into her legs with a

vengeance. Sarah looked at his bent head and wondered what he was thinking, but the promise to touch him more burned in her soul. If more of this was coming later, she wanted to get the day moving!

Laying the lotion bottle aside, Reagan sat back on his haunches. "That's about as much protection from the sun as possible." With a hop up, he grabbed her hands and helped her stand. There was a deliciously wicked look in his eyes, and he had that little boy look to him again. Sarah couldn't even begin to guess what he was thinking.

"You know what we need right now?" he asked with a silly grin on his face.

"No...what do we need right now?" She answered him with both hands on her hips and a light in her eyes.

"A race!" Reagan yelled. Saying that, he popped her on the rear end and ran for the beach like all Hell was after him.

"Hey, no fair! You got a head start!" Laughing and rubbing her behind, Sarah scrambled after the boy in a man's skin. Reagan headed straight for the water, ran out a ways then dove into the waves. Sarah was right behind him. Both came up for air within a few feet of each other. A game of splash ensued, and for the next hour, they played, dived, chased each other and generally had a grand time. However, for as many times as they chased each other, neither one of them ever caught the other.

The moment was building. The time wasn't just right yet. But something was definitely coming.

———

Sarah jumped for a seagull then stood with her arms thrown wide. Throwing her head back and giving a large sigh, she fell backwards into the waves. She was having a wonderful time. As she pulled herself up from the bubbling water, she felt

Reagan's arms wrap around her waist and assist her up. She came out of the waves with water streaming down her face from her hair. Shaking the salty water out of her eyes, she realized she was standing with her arms around his shoulders, and he held her to him tightly. His face was very serious, and there was a question in his eyes.

Sarah didn't know what Reagan wanted, but she knew what she wanted. Pulling his head down to her, she kissed him, opening his lips with gentle pressure and exploring the salty interior of his mouth with her own. She didn't grasp and grab nor rush the moment.

It wasn't until she realized that Reagan was kissing her back that they both knew something special was afoot. The kiss was delicate and sensual. It developed from exploratory to possessive. Both stopped before that meeting of flesh turned carnal. But there was a promise of more to come. Each looked at the other with the understanding that there *would* be more.

"Enough for the moment," Reagan whispered. "I'm a strong man, but you make me weak, and we can't have that," he teased with another soft but quick kiss. "Besides I'm slowing down," he said as he released her slowly, letting their hands move apart like in the movies, inch by inch. He moved toward the beach and called back over his shoulder while he waved her in. "And you're tuckered out."

Though she protested, Sarah heaved her body out of the water, only then realizing Reagan was right. Pulling her body out of the water felt like lifting a ton of bricks!

They waded out slowly, giving each other time to regain physical and emotional control. It was a matter of time now, no need to rush. They could take it slowly. What would come later would be the sweeter for the waiting.

Reagan waited on the sand for her, his arm out to wrap around her shoulder as she stepped up to his side. A chill passed over Sarah's back as they neared the umbrella.

"Let's get you warmed up." Reagan grabbed a beach towel and briskly rubbed her down, clowning so that she laughed rather than be embarrassed as he deftly dried off more intimate places. He ran the towel over his body, tossed it over a low branch, and plopped down on the beach blanket and lay back on the pillow. "Join me?" He raised his hand to her, his eyes inviting her to join him. He wiggled a shoulder. "I've got a well-muscled shoulder you can lay on."

"Can't resist an offer like that." Sarah went down on her knees, stretched out next to Reagan and wiggled around getting comfortable on that muscled shoulder.

But he stopped her with a hand on her hip. "I have lots of patience and control, Sarah, but let's not push it too far too fast. Okay?"

She realized her wiggling was re-igniting the fire that began burning in the cool waters of the blue Australian ocean. Nodding her head to show she understood, she laid her head on his shoulder and quietened.

Once settled, they seemed to drift off into a comfortable silence again. One that didn't last long. Reagan was anxious to know more about Sarah, just as he said earlier.

"Sarah, tell me what you meant by knowing about my photos but not the man. You teach writing. What does that have to do with my pictures?" Reagan lay with his eyes shut, but Sarah knew that lively mind was coming up with more questions than she might be able to answer all in one afternoon. Reagan snuggled her body closer to his and popped one eye open as he waited for her answer.

"Let's see, where to begin," Sarah mused. "Parents deceased. No siblings. Just a few houseplants and me near the campus. I teach creative writing at Princeton like I mentioned before. It's a popular course, and every class is as full as the Dean allows. I guess that's because of how I teach the students to write. Of course, these kids can write, but they limit themselves...they don't use their imagination. That's where I bring in music, movies and your photographs, Reagan. Your pictures are all over my classroom and my office. The students have seen that video of your photos with your narrative."

At that, Reagan opened both eyes and glared at her. "You've *got* to be kidding! That damn thing? I only did it because the publisher was driving me fucking daft, and I wanted him off my back before I left again. I can't believe anyone ever watched that thing!" Reagan lay back down, shook his head and snorted in disgust. "You're really hard up for something to show your class, woman," he grumbled.

Sarah laughed and swatted his hand that waved in the air as he groused about the video. "Do you want me to continue or not, sir?" Sarah pretended to be angry with him, but both knew she wasn't really.

"Oh, pray continue, fair lady." The gallant knight didn't even bother to raise his head from the pillow.

"Thank you, kind sir!" Sarah said sarcastically...but with a touch of humor to take the edge off her comment. "Anyway, I show them a picture of yours and have them write about it. Then other times I use music. I usually use the Beatles and N'Sync because they're pretty straightforward with their lyrics. I use Coldplay when I want the kids to *think*." She also mentioned a small band from Australia.

"Who?"

"Weren't you born in Oz? Don't you know who they are?" Sarah was flabbergasted. "They're one of my favorite groups, and you don't know them? I can't believe it." His ignorance truly astonished her, but she was in for a surprise.

"Get a hold of yourself, woman! I was just funning. Of course I know who they are...their front man is an actor, isn't he?" Reagan scooted into a more comfortable position and readjusted Sarah's head slightly on his shoulder. "Geez, can't a man make a joke?" Though he sounded wounded, Sarah could tell by the way he was grinning that he was pulling her leg.

"Okay, laugh if you will, but when I want the kids to think about what a band is singing, what the lyrics are saying, I play their music. There's nothing straightforward about that bunch. And their front man...well, he was at Princeton several years ago doing a movie. Turned out to be a good one. I saw it several times. But when he was on campus for those few weeks, he created so much havoc with my students! Lord, the girls were late for class...if they came to class at all, and they mooned over him all the time and talked about him constantly. Don't get me wrong. He's one of *my* favorite actors too, but he was making a mess of my class. Oh, and on top of that, the film company asked to use my 1948 MG touring car for him to drive in several of the shots. That was pretty cool."

"Finally, though I just put a picture of him up on the computer overhead and told the class to write an essay—totally fiction—using the physical characteristics of the man but without using the real man, his name, job or anything else. Boy, you should have read some of *those* essays. I have to admit though, some of those kids did a great job using that man as a starting point for their stories. I also work with a publishing company where I send some of my own stories and those of some of my more promising students. I submitted a few of *those* particular stories for publication, with the kids' permission of course."

"A MG touring car? Bloody ripper!"

"What?" Sarah raised her head, confused. "Is that good or bad?"

"Huh? Oh...Aussie-speak for awesome, love."

"Okay then." She laid her head down and wondered how a person could say something in English that meant nothing like what the English meant it to be. Or at least American English.

"So did the actor chaos ever calm down?"

"It's funny...I guess he heard about the problems he was causing my class and how I had channeled that energy because he stopped one day on his way home for the evening. We were both running late, and we met just as he was getting into his Suburban to go home. He apologized for interrupting my classes but applauded me for getting round it. He also thanked me for letting him use my car. It's the only thing I really value besides my teaching. We talked for a few minutes, but I could tell he was really worn out, so I wished him well, told him I looked forward to seeing his film, and advised him to go home and get some sleep. He laughed but did get in the car and leave. I admire his talent and his dedication. But I was glad to see him go! Later he sent a lovely, autographed picture over to me with a little note. I framed the photo and note and put it up in my office next to your picture."

Sarah was half-asleep by the time she finished telling her tale and let that last part slip. She didn't mean for Reagan to know that his picture was in her office. She hoped he hadn't heard that.

"What's your favorite picture, Sarah?" Reagan asked sleepily. When she didn't answer, he looked over at her. "What's the matter? I really want to know...what picture do you like best of all the ones you've ever seen...mine or anyone else's for that matter." He closed his eyes again, but he nudged her to make her answer. He was so laid back about it all that she figured she had nothing to lose so she answered honestly. She also realized he hadn't heard her comment about having his photo in her office.

"Actually, my favorite picture *isn't* one of yours." Sarah got a reaction out of that statement.

"Really? Dang, whose picture is it then?" Reagan sounded disappointed.

"Well, if you must know, it isn't a picture *by* you. It's a picture *of* you." That got the reaction she expected.

"What did you say? No one's ever taken a photo of me...at least none I've ever seen." Reagan sat up so quickly she got jostled off his warm shoulder.

"I know...I know. You hate having your picture taken, but one of your Sherpa snapped this one as you were heading up some kind of mountain evidently. He caught you as you turned around to look over your shoulder at something beyond him. It's from your right side. There's a fierce look of concentration on your face and frown lines on your forehead. You were totally unaware of the man and the camera. That's not like you to be so unobservant. So I figured you had a lot on your mind." While she talked, Sarah pulled Reagan back onto the pillow, touched his forehead and smoothed her fingers over the place where those worry lines often showed up. He tilted his head up and kissed her palm. She smiled and laid her hand back on his chest, right above his rapidly beating heart.

"Where ever did you get *that* picture? *I've* never seen it," was all he had to say on the subject.

"Oh, your agent is friends with my publisher, and the agent knows I like your work, so she sent me a copy of the picture, making me promise I wouldn't sell it to the magazines or whoever. It was a great temptation, let me tell you, Reagan, because the photograph is a good one. But I couldn't see sharing you with the world, so I kept my end of the bargain. I got the best part of the deal too, if you ask me."

"Too right. I'll have to see this masterpiece some day, you know.

Chapter Three

Sarah wanted Reagan awake so she played with him. First a tickle on the side of his leg. He moved the leg but that didn't wake him. So she did it again. This time he turned over but surprised her by waking and pinning her under him. She squealed with surprise when he woke in a playful mood.

"And just what was that I felt?" Reagan kept her hands pinned above her head. Sarah could hardly speak, she laughed so hard.

"My toes, silly man. What did you think? That a crab or something was climbing over you?" That set her off to giggling again.

"You interrupted a perfectly perfect dream of me and you. So what's so important that you did that, huh?" He tried frowning, but she knew he wasn't serious because he worked hard to keep a grin from lifting his lips.

"I'm starving!"

To punish her for disturbing his sleep, the man kissed her only once before sitting up and running his hands through his hair then rubbing both eyes with his fists like a little boy would do. Sarah thought that was a very endearing gesture.

"I'm dying of hunger here. What did you pack in that cooler? Something good, I hope." She sat with legs pulled up in Indian style and watched as he pulled the cooler over to them. Out came chicken and beer along with cheese, various vegetables and fruit.

"Wow, a regular banquet." She pulled out plates and silverware as well as two glasses.

"The lady that takes care of the house keeps a fully stocked 'frig." He piled several things on a plate and passed it to Sarah. Popping the top on beer, he held it up to her. "You want your coldie in a glass or from the bottle?"

"The bottle is fine." She had to swallow a delicious bite of cold chicken leg before she could answer. "Man, this is great."

"She won't be back before I leave so I won't be able to thank her in person." He rummaged through the cooler when he said he was leaving. Sarah carefully schooled her expression so as to not show her dismay. They had a weekend for sure. Beyond that was a dream. A dream that would end at the end of the weekend apparently. No sense letting him see how much her heart was breaking.

They spread the feast out on the blanket and opened a beer apiece. With the fresh breeze off the water and a relaxing nap behind them, they ate as if they had never seen food before in their life. Reagan picked up the conversation they let drift when they both went to sleep.

"So if I'm your favorite picture, what's your favorite song? Something by that Aussie band?" He wiggled his eyebrows and made a face when he asked.

"You're teasing me, I know so I'll ignore that face you're making." She reached out and tweaked the end of his nose. "Actually, my favorite song is by the Beatles, Mr. Smarty," she replied. "The Long and Winding Road. Ever hear of it?"

"Of course!" Reagan shot back in faked indignation. "What do you take me for? A hermit? Everybody's heard that song...it's on the <u>One</u> CD, but it's an old song. What's so special about that one?"

"Well," Sarah said as she leaned over and wiped a blot of mayonnaise off his nose, "you always hear that it's the journey that's important rather than the destination." He nodded in agreement and grunted. "But it seems to me that once in a while, it's the destination that makes the journey worthwhile...like going through life but finally finding something of great value at the end of the road. I don't know how to explain it exactly, but what if your heart yearned for something and you looked for it forever and then at last, you found what you wanted. A person would certainly have moments of torture and pleasure along the way, but wouldn't it make the whole journey worth the effort if a person found his heart's desire waiting at the end of the road?" She plopped a piece of fruit in her mouth as she finished her explanation but watched Reagan to see what he thought.

"I've always heard that saying about the journey, but I never really gave it any thought as to *what* a person might be traveling *to*. Makes sense, I guess. I'll have to think about that." He rustled around in the cooler again and came out with small pieces of some kind of cake. He passed a piece to Sarah. "I like the sounds of Metallica! I generally don't have a lot of free time for music, but when I do, they're the ones I like to listen to the most."

So saying, he wadded up his napkin, shot for the cooler, made the shot then lay his head down on Sarah's leg. He closed his eyes and laid his hands across his stomach, the image of a happy person. Here was a man perfectly at ease with himself and his surroundings.

Sarah looked down at him and decided to ask her own

questions. To get his attention, she laid her hand on his shoulder.

"You know all about me now, but I still know more about your pictures than I know about the man who took them. That's not fair." Sarah lowered her voice. "Tell me a little about yourself, Reagan. Please?" Absently she caressed his shoulder as she asked.

"Umm, that feels good. If you promise not to stop, I'll tell you the life history of Reagan Conley. Takes about two minutes. Mum died when I was ten. Just me and Dad then. He was a professional photographer who went through the war and survived. After Mum was gone, I lived with my aunt in New Zealand while he traveled for his journalist work. My accent mellowed because of that. He took me trekking around the world when school let out. That smoothed out the slang, and now I sound more international than Australian. I attended boarding school in Christchurch and hated every minute of it, I might add. I wanted to be with my dad. Over the years, I took over the shoots while he faded more and more into the background. That's the way he wanted it. He taught me everything there was to know about cameras, light, action. I learned on my own and added to what he taught me. Right out of school, I submitted a portfolio of my own pictures to Dad's publishing company and National Geographic. Both wanted the lot. I've been taking photos and doing the journalism that goes with them ever since. I still stick with the same publishing company and agent. Dad died about ten years ago. Since then, I've been all over the world several times. I've seen more barroom fights than the law allows. I've frozen in temperatures no sane person should be in and blistered from heat that dries the body within three days. Damn near died on several occasions. I'm between jobs right now, but I leave Monday morning for India and the Himalayas. And that, my darling, is the life of Reagan Conley. Happy?" The man told the short tale of his life without even opening his eyes.

"But Reagan, there's so much more to the story! You were trapped between two flows of lava about two years ago. Before that, a blizzard stranded you on Mt. Everest. And then there was the time when you missed the pickup in the desert and almost—"

Reagan turned over and put his hand softly over Sarah's mouth.

"What's the matter? Trying to scare me to death? Sure, those things happened, but it's not like death comes calling on me every day. Most of the time I'm as safe as a baby in his own crib. Don't worry about me...I came out all right." Despite the fact that his hand prevented her from speaking, he could tell she still wanted to argue the safety of his job. "Make you a deal. We won't talk about our jobs anymore, and in return, I'll take you on a long walk down the beach. How's that?"

Reagan removed his hand as he talked, but still leaned on one elbow with his face close to Sarah's. When she still looked like she was going to draw breath and argue, he kissed her quickly on the lips then rolled away from her. Surging to his feet, he offered a hand to help her up. "Let's walk some, okay?"

She couldn't resist him when he looked like that. Accepting his offer of a hand up, she stood. Together they packed the food in the cooler. She slipped the T-shirt on over her panties and bra while Reagan grabbed his camera. Laying his arm across her shoulders, he guided her down the beach. She wrapped an arm around his waist and followed his lead.

They walked a long time. Sometimes they talked. The wind off the water cooled, and Sarah's hair became tangled. Reagan threw pebbles across the waves, snapped pictures, and both dug holes with their toes only to see the water fill them in again. While Sarah watched Reagan dig up a sand dollar, chills ran down her spine.

"Cold?"

When she nodded, he wrapped his arms around her while she once again laid her head on his chest, snuggling up under his chin. "Feel better?" She nodded again. "Let's get you home. At least the wind won't bother you there." Turning back, he again put an arm around her.

The sun setting across the far side of the horizon took Sarah's breath away. It seemed as if the sun was there one minute, low in the sky, burning everything with its golden color, and then those colors faded into pinks, pale blues, corals and purples. In only a few minutes, the sun disappeared, sucked into a sea that turned from brilliant blue to a midnight black. Reagan said there'd be a moon later. Sarah looked forward to seeing it, her heart full of delight and anticipation.

Chapter Four

With the sun gone, the sand cooled quickly. By the time the pair gathered their towels, umbrella, cooler and beach paraphernalia, they could see the moon rising above the house. Climbing the stairs to the terrace, they deposited everything on the deck. Reagan set his camera on the table.

"Want a glass of wine?"

"That would be lovely. I'll stay here if that's all right. The view is breathtaking."

Reagan followed her gaze to see brilliant streamers of light racing from horizon to the shore where the moon flashed its light out at sea. "Pretty amazing. Gets to me no matter where in the world I am...the sight of the moon coming up." He grabbed up the cooler and disappeared in the house. She could hear him moving things around. The sound of the 'frig opening then closing. The clink of glasses.

She curled up on a large lounge-type chair...actually it looked more like a bed with a canvas mattress. It was quite comfortable. She pulled the pillow Reagan left on the foot of the lounge to her and propped it under her breasts as she lay on her stomach looking at the water. Though all the doors to the terrace were open, she didn't hear Reagan approach until he stood beside her. Handing a drink to her, he patted her hip, indicating she should move over so he could sit beside her.

"Salute!" he offered as he held up his glass. Touching the rim of her glass to his, they both sipped wine and watched the moon glide higher.

"You're right...no breeze here."

"The dunes protect us as well as the thick forest around here. We're fairly isolated here."

Reagan shifted and put his hand in the middle of Sarah's back. Left it there while he continued drinking the wine. A warmth spread from his hand outward across her back, down her legs and around to her breasts. That heat wasn't from the wine; she was sure of that. The heady feeling came from being close to Reagan, not from any wine she might be drinking.

Reagan watched as Sarah finished the last sip of wine then he reached over and took the glass from her hand. Setting both glasses on the floor next to the lounge, he turned his attention back to her.

The time had come.

"I want a kiss, Sarah." He eased nearer. "I want more to be honest, but I have to be sure it's what you want as well. I want..." He stopped, not sure how to say what he wanted though in his mind...in his heart...he knew exactly what he wanted.

"And what do you want, Reagan?" Sarah turned a soft gaze up to him, her hand on his leg.

"I want you to spend the night with me. Be part of all that implies. Does that scare you?" Keeping his hand in place, he scooted closer. "I see no fear." He barely breathed the words.

"No fear. Only want. Invitation. Kiss me, Reagan." Sarah reached up for him.

Slowly he bent over her and rubbed his cheek next to hers.

Pulling back, he gazed into her face. "Your eyes are so soft, so..."

Sarah's tongue came out unbidden and licked her suddenly dry lips. Fearing he might not come to her fully, she raised her hands and cupped his cheeks. Rising slightly she pulled his head toward hers. Salty lips tasted the salt on the other's lips. Heads turned to fit with each other. Short little kisses, butterfly kisses...a longer kiss that parted her lips followed by another that went on forever.

Reagan sank down on top of Sarah and curled his arms around her while she drank the passion from his mouth. Neither hurried the other. Slowly and deliberately, they enjoyed the feel of lips and touch. She brushed his lips with her soft mouth then moved on to rain little kisses over his cheek and down his neck, back up to his ear. That seemed to drive him crazy. Reagan backed away from Sarah just far enough to push the matted hair off her forehead. In his eyes, something exciting brewed, a promise.

"Around the corner is an outdoor shower. I'll wash you then you wash me. What do you say?" Reagan cradled Sarah's body, stroked her tangled salt-soaked hair and watched her with such want that she knew this was her opportunity.

"Sounds perfect," she said as she moved out of his arms. Standing up, she was the one this time who offered a hand up.

Moonlight flooded the terrace. Hand in hand, they rounded the corner of the house. A large showerhead hung from the wall about seven feet high. The railing here supported benches. In the corner stood bottles of what Sarah knew would be shampoo and soap. Maybe body lotion.

"No towels?" She gave him a coquettish look with that question.

"You won't need one."

"No, I think you're probably right." She let her gaze match his, hot with anticipation.

Reagan turned the water on, and a gentle spray fell over both of them. Pulling Sarah to him, he gathered the bottom of the large shirt she wore and worked it up her body.

She held his gaze like she was a snake charmer and he the snake. She raised her arms so he could pull the shirt over her head.

Reagan dropped the wet garment on the floor and raised his hands to Sarah's hair. The water poured over it. Reaching over to the ledge, he got the bottle of shampoo and poured a little into the palm of his hand. Rubbing them together, he again ran his fingers through the wet strands.

"Short hair that curls...too right. This is like brown satin over my hands." He rubbed her scalp with a massaging motion.

As he worked those strong fingers around her scalp, Sarah arched her body toward his. She held on to him, hands splayed out to embrace his ribs. Throwing her head back, she rubbed against him, her movements slow and sensuous.

He moved one arm down to circle her waist while the other rinsed the salt and shampoo from her hair. His pelvis ground into hers, his dick filling with blood, growing harder with each second.

Sarah pulled her head up and nuzzled Reagan's neck. He pushed her away from him just enough to look her in the eyes as he reached behind her and undid the clasp on her bra. Leisurely he pulled the garment off her shoulders and slid the straps down her arms. She moved with him and allowed the wisp of lace and silk to fall to the side.

"Did you know, love," his voice a bare croak, "that when these dainties are wet, they're almost transparent? You didn't know that, did you?" He didn't wait for her to answer. "Then you'd put that shirt back on, and all I could do was imagine what it would be like if that shirt was all you wore." He ran his hands down her ribs and followed it, his legs buckling as he knelt in front of her, taking her wet panties with him. "You're so soft. So warm. The water couldn't cool off what I've wanted ever since I saw you at that pub." He nuzzled her stomach and ran his tongue over her navel, kissing it next. Stretching up, he kept kissing her mid-section as his hands found her breasts.

Nipples hard and sensitive, Sarah thought she might die from the sensations coming from his tongue and his fingers squeezing then flicking her nipples.

He rose to one knee and gave her a look that asked permission.

Stretching her arms above her head, she gave him permission to let his mouth take over from his hands. As his mouth sucked in one nipple, she reacted by instinct, her arms coming down to clasp his head closer to that throbbing point. She rose on tiptoe and growled in pleasure as he sucked her nipple in deep, his tongue flicking it now.

He only broke the connection to move from one breast to the other, a trail of kisses chaining from breast to breast. "This one needs some loving," he managed to get out before latching down.

Sarah jumped as he nipped the end of her breast, sending jolts of desire from there straight down to her most intimate place. She tightened her embrace, running one hand through his hair, moaning in satisfaction while Reagan groaned, lost in that same desire.

Reagan surfaced for air and a touch of sanity apparently. Kissing her in a quick hard manner, he whispered, "Wait. It'll be worth it, I hope. No rush. No worries. We'll get there. First..." He once more reached for a bottle on the ledge. Seeing a question in the woman's eyes, he put his finger to his lips and motioned her to silence. Taking the squeeze bottle, he pressed open the top then stepped back from Sarah. Using his hand, he turned her around as he dribbled liquid soap all over her. The mixture was cool to the touch, and she shivered.

But he had an answer for that. Putting the bottle to one side, he moved closer to her, pulling her flush to his body. Before she could say anything, he began rubbing the soap into a foamy concoction on her back. Both hands worked on her back, moving low to her buttocks and under the cheeks of her ass. His hands slid up her back then kneaded the muscles of her shoulders before moving down her arms. Reagan held both arms out to her side as he worked the soap into her skin. But not once did his eyes leave hers. Up her neck, under her chin, behind her ears, carefully over her face, tilting her head back to rinse the soap from her eyes, down her upper chest and under her arms to return to her ass.

Reagan knelt in front of Sarah and rubbed his hands down first one leg then the other, lifting each foot and gently rubbing between each toe. She balanced herself by resting her hands on his shoulders, enjoying the feel of his muscles as they stretched and retracted with his efforts. Before he rose, Reagan ran his tongue through the curls covering her sex. Sarah almost lost it right there. She was tight already and wet with something other than water.

"How much longer?" She panted as she spoke. Or tried to speak.

"We can draw out this magic, love," he promised. Rising to meet her gaze once again, the man used both hands to lather the soap across her breasts, down her belly and finally across the most sensitive part of her body. But he wouldn't stay there between her legs like she wanted him to. He moved on, heightening her desires even more. Turning her this way and that, he rinsed the soap from her then kissed her shoulders.

"Now do me, love." was all he said to her as he used his

hands on her upper arms to move her back from him a few feet.

This time it was Sarah who lathered her companion's hair and rinsed it clean. Rubbing soap in her hands, she glanced up at Reagan through dark lashes and gave him a seductive look. Putting her palms forward, she hesitated momentarily before she touched him, but not because she was afraid. Oh no...she wondered how long it would be before she *demanded* he make love to her.

"You will make love to me...soon. But first I'll have my fun," she warned him, a wicked glance and a cocked eye signaling him of delight ahead.

Now she would touch him to her heart's content. Slowly Sarah laid her palms flat on Reagan's chest and used her thumbs to stimulate his nipples. A groan escaped him as he sucked in *his* breath. Over his chest and around the top of his broad shoulders then down to the biceps in each arm. One by one, she worked the bubbling liquid past his elbows to his hands. She massaged the fingers of each hand before kissing them, holding them up to the water, allowing it to flow down the length of his body.

Stepping closer to his body, she circled the muscles in his buttocks, then pulled him to her, matching his erect sex to the mound of hers. For a second, she ground into him like he did to her, but she pulled back when he tried to keep her there.

"Uh-uh, not yet."

Sinking to the floor, she washed his legs, reveling in the feel of the hair and muscles there. But before Sarah rose, she buried her nose in the patch of dark hair surrounding his penis. The shaft twitched as she rubbed her cheek against it. The warm flesh expanded even further. Daring much, hoping for all, Sarah raised her eyes to meet Reagan's even as she stuck out her tongue and ran it up the quivering rod of human flesh. The man above her threw back his head and clenched his fists. Oh, the power she had. The control he worked to master. Coming up a little higher on her knees, Sarah gave Reagan an enticing glance before she tongued him again. Using her hand to pull that massive appendage down to her face, she gently...sweetly...sucked the length into her moist mouth.

Groaning, Reagan managed, "I'm dying here. I swear it. What the hell are you doing to me? I'm about..." Words failed him as she swirled her tongue around him.

When Sarah released him, he caught her by surprise, grabbing her arm. He bent down and slung her over his shoulder. Moving with determined steps, he made it to the oversized lounge before bending again and laying her down. In one fluid motion, he came over her and took her mouth with his. Sarah cupped his ass to her then guided his shaft home where it belonged.

"Not slow. I'm slick, hot, wet. Sooo ready for you," Sarah moaned.

He slid in to her up to the hilt. His pelvis met her mound, and curls mingled with curls. The moisture that signaled a woman's readiness for sex flowed from her body to his, a signal that she welcomed him.

As his manhood throbbed in her and ached to find release, she lay with arched back, the better to take him in fully. He lay atop her, feeling her legs spread wider in order to take him deeper. Her hands massaged the muscles that bulged in his arms.

Throwing his head back, he began a rhythm that she found and matched. As if his body focused in just one spot, Reagan used his shaft to drive into Sarah's body.

Her body bunched around him, pulling him, drawing him further into her. The pressure built, the pace increased. Sarah couldn't help but moan as Reagan began talking sexy to her.

"You're tight and hot. Slick. Those muscles...dear God, do that again. I'm going to eat you alive when I can breathe and think again. Suck me up, love."

Sarah's mind held one last coherent thought before the thrill of old-fashion sex mixed with the magic of love took over. Jesus, will this torture of the most magnificent kind never end? Please God, never let it end.

Deeper and deeper Reagan plunged as Sarah rose up higher and higher to meet him.

———

A warm breeze caressed Sarah's cheek. Even better, warm skin lay against her back. In a mischievous mood, she wiggled just a little to see if anyone behind her was awake yet. When that big body pushed up against her ass and one hand held her tightly to him, she grinned. Oh yeah, someone was awake and hungry. And he wasn't looking for breakfast either.

"Awake, are we? Ready to eat?" She teased him with naughty thoughts that had nothing to do with food.

Reaching up for the hand that lay on her hip, she laced her fingers with Reagan's then dragged that very masculine hand to rest between her breasts. Guiding his hand, she massaged each breast then stretched as she moved his willing set of fingers lower to her belly then slowly...slowly lower to rest on the mound at the top of her legs.

Reagan's tongue started licking her back. Her smile disappeared when he moved his hand down further in to the thatch of hair and used his fingers to spread her feminine lips apart and rub her with exquisite care. Pure sexual liquid flooded her passageway, preparing it for him. Only *this* time, Sarah turned to him and rolled *him* over.

She devoured him, using her mouth, teeth and tongue to excite and torment him. She drove him past the point of madness and on to the point of that most desired moment... when Heaven calls lovers by offering them one throbbing, pounding, gripping sensation...when all reason leaves the head and only the body and heart are in control. The journey from first glance to invitation to passion was worth every minute of the wait, Sarah thought as she took him to the edge then carried him to bliss with her. The sun found the lovers where they lay, entwined around each other like two halves that finally found the other part of themselves.

The next time Sarah woke, she discovered a sheet lay over her. The smell of coffee drifted out of the kitchen where she heard silverware clattering. She barely had time to sit up, pull her legs up Indian-style and wrap the sheet around her before Reagan came out on the terrace carrying a large tray with what looked like breakfast.

"Hungry?" he asked with a smile and a kiss for her.

"Starved, but I'm going to eat first. I can have more of you later." Sarah gave a wickedly seductive giggle.

"Move your tempting self over, woman and let's eat before my talents are wasted." Reagan motioned with his head for her to make room for him on the lounge. She moved only far enough for him to put the tray down while still being wonderfully close to her. In fact, his arm rested almost down the middle of her chest. She curled around it and asked for coffee with an innocent look on her face. He grinned, rolled his arm up and pulled her head over to him for another kiss.

"Enough...eat!" he ordered.

Despite Sarah's desire to get back to eating more of Reagan, the delicious breakfast showed her that she truly was hungry—for food. The coffee was excellent, and the breakfast rolls complimented the ham and eggs. She passed on the Vegemite spread though.

"That stuff is for your pleasure. I haven't developed a taste for it yet."

"Coward," he teased her as he waved a piece of croissant covered with the revolting spread under her nose.

"Gawk. Gawk." Sarah's imitation of a chicken left Reagan in stitches.

By the time they finished breakfast and sat sipping the last of the coffee in the carafe, Reagan squirmed.

"Problem?" Sarah couldn't imagine trouble but then who knew what comes next in a relationship as short as theirs.

"No, no problem. Just a favor maybe? Would you do something for me?" Seeing her curious look, he continued. "I have a cocktail party to attend tonight...one of those mandatory functions for my agent. Would you go with me?"

"I'd be...I'd be delighted, Reagan. I'll have to pick up something to wear. Is it formal or what?" Sarah's mind was spinning. He wasn't sending her away. He wanted her to stay. Never had she been so excited in her life. It was like a dream come true...being with Reagan Conley. Even if he left Monday and never contacted her again, she would die a happy woman. Well, maybe not happy because she'd miss him for the rest of her life.

Once they made love, Sarah knew no other man would make her complete. But she couldn't tell him that. He might not be the kind to settle down. Lord knows, he hadn't settled down in all these years, and she was sure he had been given plenty of opportunities. While all these thoughts went spinning through her mind, Reagan answered her question. Of course, she missed the answer.

"It is formal if you mean do I have to wear a tux. Yes, I do. Don't care for them myself, but these people pay for my work. So there it is. Do you have something at your hotel you can pick up?"

"What? I'm sorry. I guess I wasn't paying attention. Formal? I never thought of attending any formal function when I packed to come here. Lord, I guess that means a trip to one of those outrageously expensive shops." Sarah exaggerated those words.

"You worried about that? I'm paying because I invited. But if that worries you, then we can work something out." Reagan's anxious face had frown lines all over it.

"I'm teasing, silly. It's an adventure. I can't wait!" She bounced on the lounge, and Reagan had to grab the tray with one hand and the carafe with the other.

"Careful there, Cinderella." He steadied the tray and carafe then reached for his camera.

"What the heck are you going to do?" Sarah sat straight up with both hands on her hips until the sheet tried to sink. One hand remained on her hip in a pose of indignation while the other held the sheet just above the curve of her breasts.

Ignoring her frown as more teasing—just ignoring her attitude all together—he snapped photos from every angle including behind her while Sarah grumbled about his *hobby*.

"No hobby, love. Money in the pocket and all that. What say we make this a grand adventure all day? We clean up, head to your hotel so you can change then go to this posh shop I know of. I can see a perfect day ahead of us. Matches that perfect night we just had," he added softly as he bent over and kissed her.

"Huh?" Sarah got lost in that kiss.

"Adventure? On a quest for a perfect dress." He gathered the tray and scooted off to the kitchen. "Mate, this is turning out to be a *perfect*" He emphasized the word with a goofy expression, "weekend."

After breakfast, Reagan ran Sarah into his bathroom for a shower while he showered on the terrace. She threw her bra and panties into the dryer. By the time she finished and needed them, they were ready. She dressed in his bedroom while he rummaged through drawers looking for his own clothes. For two people who met less than twenty-four hours earlier, they were remarkably comfortable with each other.

―――――

"If you'll stop by my hotel I'll put on some make-up and change."

"No need, love. You're presentable and the shop will do your make-up for this evening." Reagan drove through Saturday traffic, heading for what he called a posh shop he knew of.

"It's embarrassing, walking into a place like that in rumpled clothes. At least let me change."

"If you insist, but you look good to me." Reagan gave her a soft smile then added in a goofy voice, "But you look better in the suit you were born in." He wiggled his brows, a good imitation of a letch.

She swatted at him but noticed that he changed direction, headed for her hotel.

"Give me ten minutes. Want to come up?"

"Can we have fun while we're in your room?"

"Later, big boy."

"Darn! Okay then I'll come up and sit like a stone angel while you change." He slumped and shuffled all the way to the hotel door to indicate his disappointment.

Sarah laughed, took his hand and guided him to her room.

Chapter Five

A half hour later, after driving through a construction area, Reagan parked, opened the door for Sarah then reached in for his camera after she got out.

"What?" he asked when he saw Sarah giving him a cocked eyebrow. "So sue me...I like taking pictures!"

"I'm only teasing. Photos are your passion. I couldn't stop that if I tried," she admitted as she stopped before a black door simply marked *Elegant*. "Oh dear, now I truly feel understated," as she ran her hand down the side of neatly pressed slacks paired with a silk blouse.

Reagan put his hand on the door but stopped before opening it. "Sarah, this shop fits you perfectly. You're an elegant lady, smart, funny, charming. No worries, love."

Pushing the door open, Reagan led her into one of the most elegant dress shops she'd ever been in.

"If Princeton has a shop like this, I've never been in it. And I've been to a number of formal affairs for the university. To say I'm impressed is such an understatement," she whispered as she slipped her hand into his.

He squeezed it as a nicely dressed woman came forward to meet them.

While Reagan told the attendant what kind of party they were going to and asked for suggestions, Sarah wandered the show-room floor looking at dresses on models. What she saw pleased her. The dresses were classic, timeless designs done with fabrics and accents that brought the outfits into the here and now.

Glancing back to see that Reagan still talked with the shop hostess, she stopped to admire a case of exquisite jewelry. She knew enough to know if pieces like this did not display price tags then they were out of her teacher-salary range. Still the pieces lying on dark velvet caused a sigh that Reagan caught as he stepped to her side.

"Aren't they lovely pieces?" She leaned over so far her nose almost touched the glass above a necklace paired with matching earrings. Somewhere off to her side, she heard the click and whir of Reagan's camera. She shot him a glance but turned back to the case in front of her.

"I have to say, that set is outstanding. And I've seen some pretty fabulous jewelry in my time."

She knew he referred to jewels he photographed for several Arab princes. Pieces they gave their wives upon marriage.

"But then I think jewelry is just so much glitz and glitter until the right person wears it. That's what makes it perfect." He rested his hand in the middle of Sarah's back. When she sighed again, he patted her back. "Time's wasting, as someone famous once said."

She cocked that *oh really* eyebrow at him again and rolled her eyes.

"Miss Davis has everything you need for tonight's func-tion. Shoes, dress and make-up. She also has someone who can add fluff to all those curls you sport." He ran his hand through her curls then kissed the end of her nose. "Let's see what our fashionista has lined up for you, love." He took her elbow and guided her to the woman. "Sarah, Miss Davis will take us to a fitting room where you can try on gowns. I want to see them too...okay?" Nodding to show she agreed, Sarah followed the woman while Reagan followed.

They entered a small salon, complete with several comfortable chairs, a table where an attendant placed two glasses of wine and a small stage with several mirrors so the client could see the dress they tried from several angles.

"Sip this then slip into whatever's first." Reagan sat front and center, his camera on his knee, his finger on the button, ready to snap photos. He seemed as excited as Sarah though she worried they might not find a perfect dress.

"I'll take Miss Malloy to get her hair and make-up on first, sir. We'll be at least an hour, perhaps less. She'll return in her first gown before you know it." Miss Davis whisked Sarah away behind a closed door.

Sarah spent just less than an hour being pampered with a fresh haircut and delicate make-up. Once ready, the hostess escorted her to a dressing room almost as big as Sarah's bedroom back home. Several lovely gowns hung on a rack, waiting her attention.

She dismissed only one as too fussy for her taste. Based on the designs she preferred, Miss Davis asked the attendant to bring in two to replace the one Sarah rejected. These two were more to her taste.

What a delightful three hours Sarah, Reagan and Miss Davis shared! Sarah tried on first one gown then another. She walked the short runway in front of Reagan, turned and twirled in front of the three-sided mirror and posed as the enchanted man took shot after shot of her.

"This is lovely, Reagan, but..." she'd start.

"Not quite right, is it?" Reagan would finish.

She'd nod, Miss Davis would gesture back toward the dressing room and away they would go again.

"Better but..." Sarah would say.

"Humm," Reagan would say as he snapped a photo or two, the frown between his brows matching the small one on Sarah's face.

And off she went again.

Almost ten gowns made it to the runway. Reagan sat up and sometimes stood to take photos of Sarah as she twirled or posed in front of the three-way mirror. His jacket pocket bulged with three rolls of film already. But all ten eventually returned to the rack from which they came. Sarah wasn't disappointed. Miss Davis assured her they had a number of dresses yet to be tried. She liked every dress she tried on, but always said there was just something not quite right yet.

Reagan was looking at a selection of jewelry he had called for when Sarah walked out yet again, but this time both of them knew...this was the one. She wore a simple black sheath dress in crepe with drapes that flowed over her body like dark water. A set of multiple spaghetti straps criss-crossed her shoulders and back all the way to her waist, soft skin exposed down her spine. The front draped low between her breasts, falling into the valley between. The design of the dress allowed it to hug her bodice then flare out slightly over her hips and end just above her toes. She wore high-heeled strapped sandals that matched the dress perfectly.

"What do you think, Reagan?" Sarah ran her hand down the soft material as she asked in a quiet voice. She wore no undergarments because satin lined the dress. It was just her, the dress and the shoes. Sarah moved to the end of the short runway and descended the two shallow steps. Holding her hand out to Reagan, she said, "This is the one, isn't it? It's so...so perfect."

Reagan accepted her hand and leaned over to kiss her. "It

will be perfect when you add these to that ensemble." Walking over to the jewelry case, he picked up the long necklace and matching earrings that she admired earlier. Coming back to her, he handed the earrings to her and urged her to put them on. She did, then went up the ramp and stopped in front of the large triple mirror. Hearts the size of her thumbnail lay in her ear lobes, peaking out of the curls of her hair. They were silver with gold and black swirls on them. The earrings were elegant and suited the dress as if designed for it.

Reagan came up behind her and moved his arms around her head in order to add the finishing touch. The long necklace with a larger matching heart of silver, gold and black fell into place between her breasts just above the curve of the dress. As he fastened it, she touched it to see if the magic of it was real.

"Oh Reagan," she started, but had to stop before too much emotion welled up in her voice and eyes. "It's so grand. I feel like a queen. The necklace is amazing." She spoke in a low tone that only he heard. The attendant wisely stepped out of the room. Sarah watched Reagan's gaze in the mirror as it traveled up and down her reflection.

"Sarah." The man behind her was having difficulty saying whatever it was he wanted to say. "I've never wanted to touch someone so badly in my life."

"No," he added quickly when Sarah would have turned in to his arms. "No, we're going to wait until we get home...and then..." Reagan left the sentence incomplete, but Sarah knew what he meant. "Don't change. Wear this home?"

He fought to keep his hands to his side, Sarah realized. His fists clinched tightly in an effort to avoid touching her. Taking her hand, he guided her down the ramp and through the showroom. While he paid, Miss Davis brought a box with her clothes, shoes and other accessories in it.

"Ready, my queen?" He held out his hand to her, his

faithful camera in his other, her dress box tucked under his arm.

At her nod, he walked her out the door of the shop into a gilded afternoon sun of brilliant gold. People on the street close to them stopped and stared.

Reagan paused with his hand at Sarah's back. When he smiled in to her eyes, she saw approval. She imagined she saw love as well. She stood even straighter, her chin up, looking like a queen who accepted the adoration from her subjects as her right.

What a sight we must make. The thought ran through her mind as she paused for a second while he stood close to her, worshipping her with his eyes. After a second or two, Reagan moved forward, opened the car door, deposited the box on the back seat then turned to her. Offering her his hand, he helped seat her in the car before shutting the door with a slam that closed out the rest of the world.

———

All the way down the highway, Reagan fought to keep his eyes on the road. He drove like a man in a fog, sweating at the same time. The car practically ran on autopilot because she doubted if he had any idea of what he was doing or where he was.

Sarah saw his eyes dart back and forth, his jaw tense, his hands tight on the steering wheel. Traffic swirled around them, but even she couldn't have told anyone what was going on that afternoon.

Passion lie ahead. He knew it. She knew it.

The most desirable man in the world sat next to Sarah. He promised to give her heart's desire to her as soon as they got back to the house. Her hands itched to feel his skin. Let them glide over the smoothness of muscle.

Her dress felt too tight over her breasts. She could only

imagine what Reagan must be feeling. Then she cut her eyes over to his lap. No imagination needed. He was as needy as her if that bulge meant anything. She gave him a serene smile as she slid her hand over to rest on his leg. Then she eased it over so it lay next to that throbbing bulge. Sweat broke out along his brows. She gave him a seductive little grin.

He sucked in enough air to float a battleship. But she almost caused a wreck when she moved her hand over his crotch and cupped his fully aroused sex.

"Holy fuck! Do you have any idea what you're doing to me, woman? I can barely think enough to drive!"

"Of course I do. I know exactly what I'm doing. And I'm loving it. I want you as ready as I am right now."

"If there were a wide spot in this road, I swear, Sarah, I'd pull over and show you just how ready I am...right now!" Reagan all but shouted as he pushed the gas pedal down further "You're a wicked woman," he announced as he panted.

They left the road on a two-wheel turn then zoomed up the tarmac leading to the house. Reagan braked the car to a stop so quickly that Sarah rocked with the motion of the car. He threw his car door open, then slammed it shut as he practically ran around to her door. "Get out, woman. Right now." Grabbing her hand and snatching up his camera bag, he pulled her to the front door, unlocked it but left it as open as he had her car door as he continued to drag her through the house.

Into the bedroom he went, paused, placed Sarah in the middle of the room then walked over to the double doors. Throwing them open, he stepped back to see the effect the late day sun had on this vision before him.

"Perfect. No disappointment here with that sun at this angle. I'm hurting and so hard I don't know if I can bury myself soon enough in you but...I want this photo just as much. Maybe more. And that's saying more than you'll ever know."

Grabbing a camera from the bedside table, he stepped back near the doors and then stopped. Looking at her over his shoulder, he had to ask...just to make sure. "Sarah, do you understand how much I want to capture you on film?"

Evidently, she did because she raised her arm and pushed her fingers through her hair as she posed for his camera. Following his instructions, she moved a few times.

"Talk to me, Sarah."

"I'm going to wait, but you're going to pay for it," she teased. As she turned, she told him exactly what she wanted him to do to her, how she wanted him to remove the dress tenderly in tiny steps. Her every move was graceful. Her every glance smoldered and burned the camera. Reagan held out as long as he could before laying the camera to one side. The sun was a fiery ball on the horizon that sent probing slivers of red and orange into the room where the lovers stood.

"Love me, Sarah," he breathed in a whisper across the room.

They came slowly toward each other than halted while Reagan satisfied his craving to feel Sarah through the dress. His palms molded the fabric to her breasts, down to her waist then on to her hips.

"You suit me so well," he marveled. "Your head fits too perfectly under my chin. See?" He pulled her to him and tucked her head where he wanted her. Turning a little, he stroked her hair. "The sun is turning all those curls to copper. You remind me of a fairy—a delicate beautiful fairy."

Reagan pulled his hands out of her hair and surrounded her face in warmth. "Do you know what I see when looking at you?"

Sarah shook her head as she placed her hands over his where they cradled her cheeks.

"I see a long heart-shaped face with narrow brown brows and a straight nose that ends with a slight tip up. Your cheeks need no make-up other than what the sun adds to it. But the most captivating thing about you, love, is your eyes...hazel colored, more gold than green, clear eyes that hide nothing from me. Right now, your eyes have caught the gold of the setting sun. They shine like a twin set of topaz stones lovingly placed in the fragile beauty of your face." Words faded and Reagan removed her dress just as she asked him to—slowly with a lot of tiny kisses along the way. Once laid on the bed, nothing lay between them.

The last light of day fell across the lovers in their passionate haste to connect in the most elemental way a man and woman can. Boldly she drew his member into her mouth and swallowed it. He suckled at her breast like a babe looking for nourishment. Long after the light left the sky did they mate only to fall back on the bed in total exhaustion. Slumber claimed them for a time.

When they arose at last, both were sated physically and emotionally. Life could offer them nothing more than what each already claimed. They spoke no words about what the future might have in store.

She thought she knew what the future held, and it made her sad. He thought she could read his heart, and it made him glad. Both of them thought wrong.

———

"There's a pattern to these kinds of events. A flow," Sarah said as they pulled up to the home of Reagan's publisher. "This looks to be a big deal, Reagan." Parking valets raced back to the front door after parking guests' cars. Even now, a young man approached Reagan's side of the car, waiting patiently for him to open the door.

"I hate this kind of thing usually, but I can hardly wait to see everyone's expression when I walk in with you on my arm." Reagan gave her a wicked grin, reminiscent of the one he gave her earlier when he removed her dress.

"I've been to loads of these, and I've never had anyone remotely like you as a date. I'll have to store this night for a memory in the Princeton winter."

The valet waited while Reagan exited, closed his door then moved to Sarah's side. He held the door and offered a hand to help her stand. Once they left the car, the valet drove it sedately down the drive to disappear somewhere mysterious in the dark.

Reagan cocked his arm and gave Sarah a grin. "Tonight should be fun, for no other reason than you're here."

"Oh, you flatterer." Though she teased him, she laid her hand in the crock of his arm, and straightened, ready to enter a new world with a man she admitted—if only to herself—she loved madly. Memories would be all she'd have when this weekend was over. If she sighed and perhaps wiped a tiny tear from the side of her eye as they took the steps to the double front doors, no one noticed.

The publisher, his wife and another couple formed a greeting line inside the doors. "Reagan Conley, my god man. I've not seen you in ages. I wasn't even sure you could come tonight." The publisher gave Reagan a manly hug and hand-shake, then turned his attention to his client's date.

"Jacob Nome, this is Dr. Sarah Malloy. She teaches at Princeton University in the States and is here with friends on a short vaca."

"Sarah, Jacob is my oldest friend and the one who sends me on assignments. He pays the bills, and for that I love him."

"Sarah, you're most welcome." Jacob Nome reached out and shook her hand.

"My own publishing agent, Angela Warner, is a friend of

yours, I believe. I feel like I know you already through her."
She shook his hand, glad to see he didn't try to intimidate her
with a rugged squeeze intended to tell her how strong he was.

"Angela? Love that woman! So talented. And you're the
one who received *that* photo." He emphasized the word *that*
and gave her a wink.

"Cut it out, Jake. I know what photo you're talking
about, and it's damn sneaky of you to just hand it over to a
stranger." Reagan groused because others might think Sarah
and Jacob had a secret he didn't know about.

"Of course you know about it. I imagine Sarah here has
told you about it by now. And, yes, I'm a very sneaky person.
You should know that by now." Jacob gave them both a cat-
and-canary grin then motioned them on. "Let me introduce
Sarah. Reagan, you know Matilda, my wife, and Benjamin and
Tory Cupper." Jacob performed introductions then gestured
toward the inner rooms. "Find others to snark at, Reagan.
Wine and food will mellow him, Sarah. So glad to meet you."

"You'd think the man was an ogre from the way you treat
him," she whispered to Reagan as he escorted her to the bar, a
hand riding nicely along her waist.

"No ogre. A nice man but I can't let him think I'm soft, or
he'll be sending me to the most god-awful assignment places
you can imagine."

A glass of champagne in hand, they touched glasses and
set out to conquer the night.

————

Couples mingled and separated, returned to each other's sides
and parted again. That's how these socials worked. While
Sarah and Reagan drifted through the room, each stayed
tuned to the other. Snatches of conversation kept them
focused on each other.

"John Handley, I'd like you to meet Dr. Sarah Malloy of Princeton University in the States. She teaches creative writing and uses *my* photographs as part of her course." Reagan introduced Sarah to his agent. He kept his hand in the small of her back the entire time John visited with her.

"You poor woman, haven't you got anything better to use than this hermit's pictures?" John laughed a big belly laugh as he teased Reagan. Sarah joined his laughter with some of her own. They visited briefly before Reagan urged her to move to another person he wanted her to meet.

On around the room they traveled. Once in a while, Sarah stopped to speak with someone, and Reagan would be pulled into another group. Even while she listened to those around her, she watched Reagan and saw how others admired him. She spoke in low tones and used her hands occasionally to emphasize a point. She enjoyed the gathering more than she anticipated.

"Because you're here, I'm having a good time. I've never relaxed while at one of these affairs. I'm so alone in my work that seeing all these people in one place tends to bother me. Yes," he held up a hand to forestall whatever Sarah intended to say, "I do a lot of photos in civilization and in crowds, but that doesn't make me feel less cornered. More comfortable." He guided her to a buffet and picked up a plate while filling it with things she said she'd enjoy trying.

"I feel stable tonight. Content. Does that make sense?" he asked as he guided Sarah to a table.

Sarah had no time to address this idea of stability or contentment as those at the table drew them into a conversation already going on.

Chapter Six

It was after one o'clock in the morning...Sunday morning...before they left the party.

Sarah told him all about the people she met. "I met this man who paints. I thought he meant a house painter, then I thought he meant a professional painter, but he spray paints actors for shows like *Wicked* and *Cats*. He was very studious. I imagine actors might feel more comfortable with that kind of person rather than a jolly—ho ho person who might seem lecherous."

"Oh lord, I know just who you're talking about. Tiny little man with big serious eyes."

"Yes! He almost seemed shy."

"You'll never believe, but I met an up and coming author. She wrote a novel called *Back Water* that seems to be taking the literary world by storm." He drove with one wrist draped over the steering wheel and Sarah's hand in his.

"I've read that book! It's wonderful in a dark sinister sort of way, but as you continue reading, the characters become lighter, brighter. The situation becomes clearer until at the end it's almost as if the characters and event took on a new life!" Sarah sat back, amazed. "I'm blown away by the variety of clients your publisher represents. And your agent. Amazing men to know so many creatives. Just like you."

"I'm amazing? I'm a creative?" He turned onto the tarmac leading to the house.

"Now you're just digging for compliments. You, the man, are truly amazing in so many ways. You, the photographer, are beyond description. Your eyes see things the average person never notices much less sees value or beauty in. Creative? You add the journalism that fits your photos perfectly, and you doubt your creativity? I'm not even going there." She held up her hand, palm toward him, her face a study in moonlight and faith.

"Does this feel like coming home?" Reagan asked quietly as he parked, his arms crossed over the steering wheel, the interior of the car awash with moonlight. They'd uncovered the moon roof so the light would shine in though they left the glass closed.

"Home...there are so many sayings about home. But for now, yes, we are coming home. Tired I might add but delighted with the evening."

"Well, it's morning now." Reagan got out and came around to lend Sarah a hand in getting out. "How about a glass of wine before we call it a day?"

"Sounds perfect."

He led her into the living room, sat her in the corner of a deep ruby-colored couch and turned on the lamp that sat on the small end table. She propped one arm up on the high arm and ran her hand through her short hair. She sat with her legs curled up beside her on the soft velvet. The lamp shed a pale light on an otherwise dark room, with the double doors still closed and thin curtains blocking the moonlight.

Reagan returned with two glasses of wine and his camera

bag over his shoulder. "You look so ethereal sitting there, Sarah. May I?" He nodded to the bag.

"It's okay, Reagan. To accept you, one must accept the camera and all that implies," she said quietly.

He put his glass of wine on the other table and handed Sarah her glass. "Hold and sip but don't drink it all just yet. Please."

Quick as a wink he started taking photos. Slow moves. Nothing rushed. Nothing glaring. She held up the glass and swirled the red liquid around the cut crystal interior.

"Keep doing that, Sarah." She leaned her elbow on the arm of the couch as she swirled the wine. She knew Reagan well enough now to know he was deep in creativity. He was lost to what he was seeing in his mind's eye. Making that mental image match what he was seeing in real time. The camera whirred and snapped several times as he moved quietly around her side.

Something about the glass of wine and the light fascinates him, she realized. I don't think he even knows I'm here.

Finally, Reagan put the camera down. He opened the curtains and double doors leading to the porch before picking up his wine glass and joining her on the couch. Sarah moved her feet to the other side and snuggled up against his shoulder. Neither spoke; they just enjoyed being with each other in peace and quiet after such a lively evening.

Sarah finished her wine first. "Did I tell you tonight, Reagan, how handsome you looked?" she whispered.

"No, love. I don't believe you did." He squeezed her shoulder a little tighter.

"Umm, you looked delicious, and I wasn't the only one who noticed. Other women watched you when you weren't looking, you know," she said quite seriously but with a twinkle in her eyes.

"I didn't notice anything of the kind. You're the only one

I noticed watching me." Reagan turned slightly to smile down at her.

She gave him a sweet little kiss on the cheek but stood before he could pull her to him for more. Turning out the only light that was on in the entire house, she waited for her eyes to adjust to the moonlight flooding the room through the terrace doors. Her shoes were already off, but now she reached one hand up to a strap on her gown.

"I think I'll take a shower before bed." Saying that, she pushed one strap down then pushed the other off her shoulder. Reaching behind her back, she undid the short hidden zipper as she held the dress to her breasts. Walking away from the startled man still sitting on the couch, she let the dress fall to the floor while she held on to one strap. Laying the dress carefully over a chair back, she turned to Reagan once again.

He still sat as if made of stone though Sarah thought perhaps there was a part of him that was less than stone but becoming hard like that substance. She could see the sheen of sweat breaking out across his forehead. Turning away from him, she deliberately stretched her arms up as high as she could, drawing his attention to the full length of her body.

Rather than go to the master bathroom, Sarah surprised Reagan by heading to the outside shower. He finally caught on when she disappeared out on the porch. She heard his coat and shoes hit the floor and his camera bag hit the side of the table as he followed her outside and around the corner to the showerhead.

She was already there, stretching again as the water coursed down a body made for loving. The moonlight caught her in a study of black, silver and dark blue shadows. Sarah smiled as she heard Reagan breathing in great drafts of air, but she knew he saw magic through his camera, so she continued her shower.

He might be snapping discrete photos of her, but she knew he wouldn't be able to stay away from her very long.

"You look like a goddess, all bathed in shadows and moonlight," he whispered as he continued snapping pictures. Sarah heard him, of course. Slowly she stretched to one side then the other. Pulling her foot up, she propped it on the rail and bent to run the warm water over her thigh, down the calf, then turned to smooth the liquid over her hip, still more when she raised one arm and passed a hand down from wrist, to shoulder to breast and finally to her ribs.

By then, Sarah felt like her entire body was super sensitive to just his gaze. She longed for his touch. Stepping out of the gentle wash of water, she advanced on him. Taking the camera from his hand, she laid it to one side then turned back to him. Kissing him in short, sweet touches of lips to skin, she removed his shirt, bent down to remove his socks, then in a wanton gesture, held the buckle to his belt as she moved close enough for him to feel her breasts resting on the skin of his chest.

Reagan kissed her passionately as she continued her attack on his body. Undoing the belt, she reached for the button of his slacks. After the button gave way, she pulled the two sides of the opening wider. His briefs strained in the space, and she knew he was ready. Running her hands down the inside of the tight white material, she pushed slacks and briefs down together.

Though Reagan held her firmly by the shoulders now, she still managed to get him under the shower. As she rubbed her breasts on him, the heart-shaped necklace added friction that neither could ignore. Reagan reached for the heart that hung between her full breasts and brought it to his lips where he placed a kiss on it. Holding it in his hands, he used the chain to bring Sarah's head to him for a kiss that wasn't gentle.

Passion drove Reagan, and he demanded action. Sarah answered his demands completely.

Reagan reached down and put his hands under the cheeks of her ass. Raising her to him, he let her feel his sex as it lay ready to enter her. Walking to the rail, he sat her on top and wrapped her legs tightly around him, but not before he entered her with a wild surge. Holding her butt to him and pounding away, the two went a little mad.

She threw her head back and forth, in the throes of that madness. She bit Reagan in the soft curve of his neck. It drove him crazy, adding to the crazed state he was in now.

It was as if they needed to taste and bite and kiss everything they could touch. In and out, in and out he drove. Sarah would have gone over the rail with the force Reagan used, but he held her to him and gave her a hell of a ride. When they climaxed together, Sarah wrapped her whole body around him in such a grip that she wondered if he could breath. Neither seemed to breathe for what seemed like hours. Then they melted softly into each other.

Picking up the heart necklace once more, Reagan ran it over her skin in delicate strokes. Sarah lay with her head buried in the man's neck. This was how it all started...in a bar somewhere in time and space...she with her eyes covered in the warm skin and masculine scent of this man...he with his arms around her, protecting her from that which might harm her. She prayed it would continue for a lifetime but feared she only had this weekend.

————

Sarah heard Reagan whispering in her ear early the next morning, but she was so comfortable that she only caught a few words of what he said.

"...breakfast...newspaper..."

She knew when he rolled out of bed because he left a cold spot where she had been snuggling up to his warmth. Burrowing back in to the feathery softness of the pillow, she breathed his scent then drifted back to sleep with a faint smile on her face.

"Sarah. You awake?" Someone called her, but she was so comfortable that she didn't want to open her eyes.

"Sarah"

Reagan probably thought her asleep, she wasn't. Only had her eyes closed and kept her breathing shallow and regular.

What is he up to now, she wondered.

"Wake uuuppp, sleepyhead. Your breakfast is getting cold, and it would be a shame to waste this perfect cup of coffee." Reagan's voice was enticement alone.

The smell of food and fresh coffee was more than enough to make Sarah open her eyes to a glorious sight. She stretched and smiled at Reagan who stood by the bed with two bags in hand and a large newspaper tucked under his arm. He wore a ratty looking T-shirt and shorts with no shoes.

"Oh, but you look wonderful." She sat up and pulled him carefully to her so she could kiss him. "Why is it men wake up looking as delicious in the morning as they did when they went to bed the night before? It's not fair. I bet I look like a hag." She playfully grumbled as she reached to the foot of the bed for the shirt Reagan threw there the day before. It went with one of his suits. The pressed collar still stood up, but the long sleeves hung well past her fingertips.

"Here, let me roll those up, or you'll drag them through your food." Reagan laid the sacks and paper down then reached over to perform this service for her. Having finished, he stood back to admire the pretty picture she made sitting there wearing his shirt which she didn't bother to button.

Sarah reached over and picked up the necklace where she'd put it the night before, safe on the bedside table. Leaving the earrings, she slipped the long affair over her head then reached for one of the bags.

A sigh escaped Reagan and drew her attention. "You like that necklace, don't you?"

"It has meaning. There are a lot of memories attached to it," Sarah admitted, her cheeks flushing as she sat in the middle of the bed in nothing but a man's shirt and necklace.

A kiss and a waving gesture satisfied her as she moved over so Reagan could join her. They propped up against a pile of pillows, took a coffee and bag of pasties apiece then divided the newspaper.

Sunday morning passed in a lazy day way. They sat side-by-side eating muffins and drinking large cups of coffee while sharing the articles they enjoyed or found interesting. Sarah read bits to him while he told her he always looked for what was happening in the world. If there was action going on, that's where he needed to be with his cameras.

At one point in the morning, he made a random statement that he needed to pack his old streamer trunk

"My camera equipment and the few clothes I haul around with me go in there. Keeps my things as safe as possible. That trunk usually gets to my destination ahead of me," he groused as he turned to a new page. He missed Sarah's expression, one filled with sadness and love.

"Do you leave when the trunk does?" She had to know how much time they had left.

"No, uh, no. I'll pack the trunk this afternoon, and the company picks it up tomorrow morning early. I guess that's why the dang thing gets there before me," he joked. "My plane leaves at noon. We'll have to be up early in order to gather your things and get you safely back to the hotel."

Again, he missed Sarah's anguished expression. When she used the edge of the sheet to dab a tear from her lashes, he missed that as well. Her heart fell at the reminder of how little time they had left. Less than twenty-four hours.

Reagan regaled her with stories all morning as they shared the bed for something other than passion. Somewhere that morning Sarah forgot about Reagan leaving.

———

By now, Sarah was so used to Reagan getting his camera out and taking shots that she didn't take special notice that he photographed her as she held her coffee cup and read the newspaper that lay scattered all over the bed covers. She sat with her legs tucked up Indian-style, her hair tousled in curls and pushed behind her ears, or the open shirt that suggested a glimpse of breasts without actually revealing them. The long silver, gold and black necklace hug low between her breasts. It showed plainly in the stretch of bare skin in the opening of his shirt. Fortunately, the shirt gathered around her bottom so any picture he might get would be sexy as Hell without being risqué.

Sometime in the early afternoon, Sarah wandered into the kitchen and prepared a light lunch, which they ate at the table on the terrace. The two talked about everything. Sarah talked about growing up in the South but getting a scholarship to Princeton. The university later asked her to teach creative writing. Her parents died while she was in college. With no brothers or sisters, she was on her own.

"Any serious relationship?" Reagan asked casually but she could tell he was deadly serious.

"Oh, I went out with a few men. Several were quite attractive, but nothing ever came of our times together. None ever made me want to stay with them."

Like Sarah, Reagan admitted he'd dated a few women over

the years. He refused to talk about any of them, using her own words: *None ever made me want to stay with them.*

While Sarah brought the dishes back inside and cleaned up the kitchen, Reagan set up his tripod and camera out on the deck.

"The light's good today, not glaring but muted by those banks of clouds that roll by. Sarah, when you finish in there, come out here please." When he thought she'd been inside too long, he called, "Come out here."

"Bossy man, whatever do you want," she grumbled as she returned to the deck, still wearing nothing but the oversized white shirt and necklace. The breeze ruffled the shirttail around her thighs, but the two buttons that she closed at the bottom of the shirt kept her modesty in place. Not that modesty was a concern of Sarah's, but it made her feel more enticing.

"Mmm, just how I like you best," Reagan said as he pulled her forward for a quick kiss. He sat her aside though and finished his preparations.

"What are you doing?" Sarah watched him run a long length of wire from the camera to the railing.

"This is a trip line that will trigger the camera shutter when I click it," he explained. When he had the equipment set up like he wanted it, he came to her and pulled her into his arms. She snuggled with him as he confessed to her, "I'm selfish. When I leave tomorrow, I want to take something with me that I can look at until I decide what to do with the rest of my life. I don't want to forget you. I want to remember every detail of your face and form. The only way I can do that is use my skill as a photographer and capture your essence on film. No photo can substitute for the real thing, but this is as close as I can get." He pushed her curls off her forehead and gave it a soft kiss. "What do you think? A photo of us together?"

"I'd like that myself," was her reply. She didn't have the

courage to ask for a copy. He was headed for parts foreign to her and possible danger. Getting one photo back to her was far down on his list of things to think about.

Placing her next to the rail with the beach at her right side, Reagan came to her far side away from the camera. Laying his cheek next to her temple, he wrapped an arm around her. Asking her to look at the water, he used the trip switch to snap the shot. Stepping back for a minute, Reagan looked at Sarah in her oversized shirt and long necklace. Assessing the possibilities, he pulled the shirt back from her chest just a little, so the necklace lay in sight. Again, he snuggled up to her and snapped the shot. Several more times he arranged the two of them for a picture.

"That's as good as I can get, love." Once more, he gave her a quick kiss, this time on the end of her nose. "Time to break all this down and store everything in that trunk." He took the equipment apart and carried it to the living room, Sarah right behind him.

He pulled out a battered steamer trunk and began placing equipment in special compartments evidently made for each one. As he worked, he showed Sarah a camera, a flash, sometimes a lens and explained how it worked. It was fascinating to hear him talk. She could have listened to his low velvet rumbling voice all day long. But when he talked about something he loved, like his work, his voice took on an extra vitality. Sarah could tell he loved what he did.

Her heart sank a little. There was no way she could ask this wonderful man to give up an adventurous life and settle in one place. She supposed she could travel with him, but she would miss teaching. It was a hopeless situation as far as she was concerned. She pushed the thoughts of Reagan leaving her to the back of her mind.

"Okay, so that's all the important stuff. Now for the less important..." he gave her a wicked grin. "Clothes. I can live without them, of course. You'd like that, but best I keep some modesty." His laughter filled the bedroom. Sarah returned to the middle of the bed and began gathering newspaper pages.

He started pulling his clothes together and laying them on the foot of the bed.

"You said you'd take enough for modesty's sake, but, Reagan, that's not a lot of clothes."

"You thought I was pulling your leg? Beyond socks, underwear, jeans and a few shirts, I either buy where I am or live in what I brought. You have to admit, some of the places I've gone on assignment don't allow for a lot of time to change clothes. Mt. Everest doesn't exactly have shops where I can buy."

"I guess that makes sense. You can't haul an entire wardrobe of clothes around the world unless you're safe and among the civilized. Which you sometimes aren't," she pointed out.

"Don't I know it."

She helped him keep the conversation light. Packing his personal things didn't take near as long as packing his equipment had.

"There! That's it. All packed. What about another swim?" He stood with hands on hips, his steamer trunk closed and latched for safety.

"Sounds great."

"And you have such a perfect outfit for swimming too," Reagan said as he fingered her bra and panties where they lay folded on the dresser.

Donning the black bra and panties, she met Reagan on the sand at the bottom of the stairs. She still had on his white shirt though. Reagan still had a camera in his hand.

"I thought you packed all those?" she asked when she saw the small camera in his hand.

"Nope, I always have at least one camera handy. I can put

this one in my carry-on bag. You never know when you might find a good shot." Reagan draped his arm over her shoulder and kissed her forehead. "We can swim down the beach a ways. But let's see if you can find something to take a picture of while we walk first."

Reagan's offer to show her how to take pictures surprised her, but once she thought about it, she realized that he wanted to share something that was important to him with her.

"What a wonderful compliment. Thank you." She ducked her head, surprised, a little embarrassed, delighted and at the same time, sad to know they only had until sunup.

Seagulls dipped above waves that made ripples in the sand. Sarah knelt to take a picture of those ripples as the water rushed back to the ocean. A pile of driftwood attracted her attention later. Several times, she stopped to snap a picture. Reagan complimented her on her good eye for visuals. A few times, he pointed out something to her and showed her how to look at the shot from various angles to determine which would be best. Other times he talked to her about being ready for the unexpected. He usually mentioned that right after a great photo opportunity passed her by. Reagan never snatched the camera from her hand though or groused about the missed shot.

She was thankful for that. Once in a while, they would stop, and he would hold her to him, letting her head rest on that broad chest while he talked. That was the part she liked the best, leaning on him while that deep voice echoed through his bones to her ear.

In her dreams, she would be able to hear him for the rest of her life. She clung to him at times a little harder, drawing out the moment for memory's sake.

Chapter Seven

They shared a quiet dinner that evening on the deck, the breeze a little cooler than the nights before. The end of May in Darwin moved closer to the cooler weather where June in the states, back at the university, would be moving into the hot summer months.

The sun hadn't set yet, still had a way to go before disappearing for the day. Sarah got quieter and quieter, but then, so did Reagan. Each held their own thoughts to themselves rather than sharing. Sarah pushed her food around the plate until Reagan reached over and took it away from her. Taking her hand, he led her to the rail and embraced her as he leaned against the thick top board.

"I don't have to ask what the matter is. I know. I'm leaving tomorrow. You're leaving the day after that. Leaving...but not together. I'm headed to Asia, and you're headed back to Princeton where it's safe. I can't even tell you if my destination is safe or not. You'll fly in one direction, and I'll be flying in the other. Sucks." He held her face and scanned her face. "This is tearing me apart, Sarah. I can see that it's not easy for you either. I assume we're good."

Oh, if you only knew, Reagan, how much I'm not *good*. I'm dying here. Sarah never took anything for granted. She was the one who always needed to be told something was right or wrong. All her colleagues at Princeton knew that, and her students learned that about her after dealing with her. She never assumed that good things would come to her. So here she stood, with a heart full of love for Reagan Conley but knowing he was leaving her forever.

Tenderly Reagan kissed Sarah's eyes, forehead, each temple, her ears, working his way to those lips that parted as if eager for his tongue to mate with hers. Her arms encircled his neck while her fingers filled her palms with his hair. Reagan pushed his hands under the edge of her shirt and rubbed her back as he kissed her again and again. Breaking the kiss, he led her through the double doors to the bed. Laying her down on the cool sheets, he made slow sensual passionate love to her.

This time she rode on top of him and sucked his staff deep into her womb. Her skin glistened with the sweat that cooled quickly after climax. Their bodies carried the smell of loving.

She slept for a brief time. When she awoke, she lay sprawled on the bed but alone. Looking around for Reagan, she discovered one of those moments in time he talked about earlier. The man she loved stood on the deck at the rail silhouetted by the sun's fading light on the horizon. He was as naked as the day he was born. Sarah's heart jerked with desire, but she reached for the camera on the nightstand. Snapping the shutter on the camera, she wondered if she'd ever see that picture. Then she realized she didn't *need* a copy in print; she would carry that scene in her heart forever.

The sun set for the last time for Reagan and Sarah. He returned to bed, letting his naked skin lay against hers. But comfort was what they needed that night, not sex or passion. They slept in each other's arms, afraid to let go for fear the night would steal one from the other.

Morgan's Express came at nine o'clock to collect Reagan's steamer trunk. He and Sarah dressed and ate before the men came to take his trunk away. Both shared funny stories and mundane conversations.

Neither said what was in their hearts though they should have.

At the last minute, they couldn't find the necklace. The earrings lay on the bedside table, but the necklace was missing. They tore the bedroom apart. Then they moved to the rest of the house and deck. Sarah broke down when they had to give up searching. That necklace was her only link to Reagan, and now she couldn't find it.

An hour passed before her face returned to its usual color. Before her tears dried. Before she could speak without falling apart again. Reagan seemed to understand and simply held her.

Dressed once again in her jeans, polo shirt and tennis shoes, Sarah carried the box from the dress shop out to the car. The eloquent black gown was lovingly packed in there as well as Reagan's white shirt that Sarah tucked in at the last minute. She almost packed it in Reagan's travel bag, but when she held it, she brought it to her nose and inhaled the scent of him. She couldn't put it among his things, so she smuggled it out in hers.

Reagan checked the house one last time, wrote a note to the housekeeper thanking her for everything, asking her to look for the necklace as she tidied up, then locked the door. He slid the key back into the mail slot in the door and joined Sarah in the car. He would leave the rented car at the airport. Neither spoke all the way to town, but Sarah sat as close to Reagan as possible. They held hands in a grip that hurt.

Parking the car and collecting their things, Reagan

arranged for a taxi to pick up Sarah. He checked in his carry-on bag and left the box with Sarah's gown with the porter. Checking in at the ticket counter, he confirmed his flight that would leave in thirty minutes. Still holding Sarah's hand in a firm grip, he walked with her down the long corridor leading to the waiting lounge. When Reagan would have sat, Sarah shook her head.

"I can't sit still. Not now. I'll just wait here...close by the windows...so I can see the planes."

The boarding call came, and people around them began gathering their things. Sarah refused to look at Reagan. When they could put it off no longer, Reagan took her by the shoulders, turning her to him. The look on her face told him everything. She was one second away from breaking down. He gathered her close, for the last time tucking her head up under his chin. Her arms went around his chest, and her hands clung to his back.

"You're so soft. I'll miss that. This is the hardest thing I've ever done. Sarah, Sarah, look at me," he begged. She wouldn't lift her face to him. He finally had to pull her face up so he could look her in the eyes. "Think of that long and winding road, Sarah. Remember the song, Sarah. Think about that song...remember the journey and the destination? Remember it, Sarah."

He held her tightly as she broke into little sobs. Her face buried itself in his neck one last time while she cried.

"Remember, Sarah, remember. I will." he said as he set her from him then picked up his bag. Sarah let the tears run down her cheeks while she covered her mouth with her hand.

Now Reagan was going to have to run for the plane. He had waited so long before leaving. Brushing her hand aside, he kissed her hard, turned and moved quickly away but not before Sarah heard him say, "I love you, Sarah."

Or did she imagine that? In the noise and rush, did he say what her heart wanted to hear?

Reagan disappeared from sight down the boarding tunnel, but she moved back to the windows to watch his plane, in case she might catch sight of him somehow. She never saw him again. The plane backed out of its allotted space, taxied down the runway, powered up then roared off into the clouds.

Chapter Eight

Apart

S arah moved like an automaton. She claimed her dress box from the porter, entered the taxi and returned to her hotel. Out of courtesy to her host and hostess, she called Sharon Bannerman while in the taxi.

"Sharon, I'm on my way to the hotel. Reagan left this morning."

"Did you have a wonderful weekend, dear?"

"More than you can imagine. But the weekend is over. He's gone west, and I'll fly east tomorrow. In the meantime, have Cary and Amy returned to the hotel? How was your weekend in Port Douglas? And flying in a private jet no less."

Sarah kept the conversation flowing so she'd not break down in more tears. Hearing the sweet elderly woman gush on about how lovely the small town was, so near the equator that the weather was warm and lovely, helped ease the pain in her heart.

"I'll be at the hotel soon. Shall we meet for lunch?"

"Come to our room first. The Petersons are here, and we can visit. Then I think we'll try The Oak for lunch. The concierge speaks highly of it. Says Oak stands for Original Australian Kitchen. Will that suit?"

"Sounds perfect, Sharon. I'll stop by my room first and change. I won't be long though."

Sarah disconnected and finished the ride staring out the taxi window, unaware of the lovely city on her last full day in Australia.

Clutching her dress box tightly she made her way through the lobby and to her room before letting a few tears drop. She quickly wiped them away and washed away any traces in the bathroom. In a new outfit with a touch of makeup, she knocked on the Bannerman's door.

For an hour, the five visited. Cory and Amy Peterson had flown to Alice Springs in the heart of Australia to visit the giant sandstone formation referred to as Uluru. Once upon a time, the Australians called it Ayers Rock, but in recent years, the name reverted to the Aboriginal name, Uluru.

"We attended a nighttime banquet out in the open with the rock as a backdrop where we tried traditional Australian dishes and listened to a star talker tell about the constellations." Cory almost whispered when he spoke of the rock formation. "You can't imagine the atmosphere there, the majesty, how inspiring the place is. It's a holy place for the Aborigines."

The conversation then turned to Sharon and Harvey Bannerman who enjoyed the weekend at Port Douglas on the northeast edge of Australia that runs along the Great Barrier Reef. "We sailed with our friends to a tiny island for a few hours one day. The water is so clear! As we walked the shoreline, we spotted a tiny clown fish trapped in one of the tidal pools. Samantha, our hostess, assured us that the fish would be all right until the tide returned. Then we went to the Daintree Forest. Oh, Sarah, you have no idea how lovely that place is. We walked through it along a trail that came out onto a huge beach!" Sharon spread her arms wide. "Very few were there so we enjoyed it almost as if we had it alone."

Finally, the conversation came around to Sarah. While she'd enjoyed the adventures of the two couples, she'd dreaded the time when they turned to her and ask about her weekend.

"Sarah, you actually met your idol Reagan Conley right here in Darwin. How perfect." Sharon lifted her eyes in a faked swoon. "Did you have a lovely time with him?"

How she wanted to evade answering. Sarah tried to tell the four what a life-altering weekend she experienced, but the words wouldn't come. Instead, she burst into sobs that frightened her four friends. She only pulled herself together because she realized how much she upset the ladies. Cory Peterson and Harvey Bannerman squirmed in discomfort but, like their wives, had no idea what was wrong.

"I'm sorry. I'm sorry." Sarah held up a hand, palm out, in an attempt to assure her companions that she was all right. "I had the most wonderful few days of my life, and it's over, and all I have left are memories." At that, the two ladies glanced at each other and sighed.

"All that love you've stored up over the years of looking at his photos and watching that video turned into the real thing this weekend. Am I right?" Sharon laid her hand on Sarah's leg, seeking some way to ease what was obviously a case of unrequited love.

"I'm not sure. Maybe. Probably," Sarah stumbled through possibilities. Finally she slumped in her chair, head down, handkerchief wadded in one hand. "Yes. But no one can do anything about how I feel. He has a job to do, and so do I."

"But you love him, and he loves you." Sharon said the obvious plainly.

"I honestly have no idea what he thinks or feels, Sharon. We had such a good time together. We laughed and talked." She left out the other activity they indulged in a great deal over those days. These people were smart enough to figure that part out on their own.

"I wish we could help, Sarah," Amy Peterson sat next to Sarah and reached over to hug her. "Perhaps this will work itself out, and he'll return."

"That would be lovely, but I'm not holding my breath, Amy. It's a great dream though." She blew her nose, wiped off the tears and offered a weak smile. "We did have a fabulous time Saturday night though at a party thrown by his publicist. I met so many interesting people." In order to take the attention off her heartbreak, she gave a fantastic view into the evening she and Reagan shared.

By two o'clock, the conversation stopped when Harvey's stomach growled loud enough to hear. "How embarrassing, folks. I think that means it's time to eat."

The group hailed two taxis and headed off to The Oak restaurant. When they returned, the older couples went to their rooms for a nap while Sarah returned to hers in order to pack. Her plane left early the next morning. The Bannermans and Petersons were staying a bit longer. She'd say her goodbyes to Harvey, Sharon, Cory and Amy before bedtime that night. She'd be up and ready for her ride to the airport before they got up.

———

Tuesday morning, Sarah returned to the airport to board her own plane headed for the States. Craig and Amy Peterson would leave Australia later in the week, and Sharon and Harvey Bannerman would leave the week after. By the time Sarah said goodbye to her friends Monday evening, the tears were gone. But the sadness in her heart would be there for a long time.

———

The first session of summer school at Princeton University began in early June, and Dr. Malloy's classes were full. Students groaned over the assignments but loved being in her class. She demanded, bullied, sought opinions and listened. Most of all, she listened when they spoke.

Her room wasn't the typical collage classroom. It rocked! Colorful posters and pictures were scattered around the walls. Music rolled out the door and down the stately halls. By now, the other teaching staff was used to her unorthodox ways, but that didn't keep them from slamming their doors closed when one of her favorite bands played at near-full volume!

Sarah had two teaching assistants. Why, she didn't know. But they both needed jobs, and she couldn't refuse them. Danny Starling and Bridget Roper helped with the computer work and kept things straight. However, Sarah liked grading the essays herself. Everything else she let the T.A.s take care of.

"I bet your house smelled musty when you got back, huh, Dr. M?" Bridget sat at her tiny spot in the crowded office the three shared.

"Not as badly as I thought it would. I was just glad to see no one broke in and stole anything. With so many knowing I would be gone for three weeks, I worried a little about that."

"I told you I'd keep an eye on things, remember?" Danny shuffled papers as he reminded her.

"I remembered, and that's the only thing that kept me from major stress. Thank you. I owe you."

"No worries," he said then grinned. "Typical Aussie saying. I guess I picked that up from something I read somewhere."

"Yeah, or you heard Dr. M say it about a million times last semester. She even said *Crikey* a few times. That was funny. She was getting ready for the trip...reading...watching videos. I think she even took on a bit of an accent."

Sarah tossed a wadded-up piece of paper at her. "I did not."

"Bet you did, and you used several expressions so many times, your students began asking about the trip. Remember? That's how they figured out where you were going on break." Ever the brave one, Bridget aimed and hit Sarah in the top of the head. "Point to me," Bridget said as she dusted her hands in victory.

"You two are rippers," Sarah laughed as she turned back to a stack of papers that sat on her tiny space she called a desk. Around her were stacks of papers waiting to be graded.

"Huh?" Danny gave Bridget the side eye. "Have we been insulted?"

"Not so...that means you're fantastic." Sarah turned back to the stacks on her desk. "I'm stoked. How about you?"

"Translation, Doc?"

"Stoked...happy."

"Oh yeah, me too. Happy. Happy." Danny rolled his eyes but attacked his own stack of papers.

"Well, aren't we all just over the moon," Bridget commented though no one paid any attention.

———

Danny and Bridget weren't the only ones who enjoyed listening to Sarah talk about her trip to Australia, or Oz as she called it. Her teaching colleagues asked her about what she did and saw and where she went. Not one of the teaching staff in her department had been to Australia. The students in her classes even asked her about the trip when they learned she spent time there at semester break.

One day she slipped while talking to a class and mentioned that she met Reagan Conley. Danny was in the classroom at the time, and he pounced on that.

"You actually met Reagan Conley! You're crazy about him...uh, his work!" He stomped to the front of the room. "Tell us about him," he demanded. "Tell us everything."

He was so excited the students wanted to know about Reagan. They'd been in her classroom long enough to know she admired the man's work. Above the den of noise with everyone talking at once, Sarah gave in graciously. She calmed the students and gave into requests for information about meeting him...what was he really like. She'd give them a truly watered-down version of her weekend with Reagan Conley.

"Meeting him must have been earth-shattering," said a tall willowy brunette named Alice as soon as the classroom was quiet enough to speak.

"Earth-shattering? I'd call it that, yes." I met him at a pub where we both had lunch." That was a tiny white lie. Pub yes. Lunch no. More like beers.

"They have pubs in Australia? Like they do in England?"

"Australia has pubs, but they're part of the Common-wealth of Nations, those countries that were once under British rule. Regarding pubs, though, so many English settled in Australia, by choice or not, that many of their places and phrases are similar to a London setting."

"Did he take photos while you were with him?"

"Many. We spent an afternoon together in Darwin. Though he said he has lots of camera equipment, he always carries a small camera with him. An opportunity to catch a truly great shot might come along and you'd miss it if you left your camera behind, he told me."

"Does he speak funny, like the Australians in the movies?"

"He's traveled around the world so much that most of the Aussie-ness has worn off, and he's more international. That, by the way, was his word for his lack of Aussie-speak."

"He's pretty famous."

"That's true. In fact, we attended a party given by his publicist, and I met so many literary, musical and art figures that my head swam from an overload of famousness."

"Wow, you not only saw some amazing places but you met your idol." Danny summed up what the class was probably thinking.

"I did—both places and idol—and I'll never be the same," Sarah concluded the impromptu trip session. When the class ended, she noticed the girls left with dreamy expressions on their faces while the guys argued with each other over Reagan's photo techniques. She chuckled quietly; she could have told them that Reagan Conley's *techniques* worked in *all* situations!

Only Danny noticed her expression turn sad when the students left, and she handed a pile of writing papers to him to carry to the office while she got some lunch.

———

Sarah returned to her office about thirty minutes later in time to catch the end of Danny telling Bridget about the Doc meeting the famous Reagan Conley.

"Doc, we've been with you a long time now. Can we ask a few more questions?"

Sarah hung her sweater on the back of her chair, sat and swiveled toward them, wondering how much detail they might want to know. How personal would they get?

"I'll answer a few more questions." She turned toward the open window, unwilling to look them in the face if the topic turned intimate.

"Did you spend *quality* time with Conley?" Danny asked the one question Sarah knew he would. None of the students in the classroom knew her well enough to realize she and Reagan might have been more than just friends.

"Yes."

"Did it hurt when you left him?"

Her chair squeaked a little when she turned back to her teaching assistants.

She saw Bridget reach out and touch Danny's arm with a frown on her face, as if he'd gone too far. Being honest wasn't going to hurt any more than when she and Reagan parted. Besides, she trusted these two not to blab her answer over campus.

"Oh yes. The pain was more than I could bear, and I hurt still. I always will."

"We have things to do, Dr. Malloy. We'll be back in a bit."

"We d—"

"Yes, we do. Come on." Bridget all but dragged Danny out of the office.

The door didn't swing all the way shut so Sarah heard Bridget's loud whisper. "Didn't you see? I had to leave because the pain started to show on her face, and my heart was breaking for her."

———

Sarah stopped at the door to her office the next morning, attempting to catch a stray paper about to flutter to the floor. The door wasn't closed all the way so she overhead Bridget talking to Danny.

"Did you see the expression on her face as she talked? I thought she was going to cry!"

"I didn't catch it until you told me later."

"I think there's more to that story than we know. Dr.

Malloy said a few things that could only have happened if she had been with him for a *long* time, if you know what I mean."

"Don't give me that look. I'm no mind reader. Whatever you want to say just go ahead and say before she comes in." Danny sounded frustrated.

"I think Dr. Malloy and Reagan Conley spent time together, and it developed into something very special. I have a feeling Dr. Malloy fell in love with him."

"Huh? Yeah, and then he left, and now she has nothing. What a bum! He just walked off and left her! And...and Dr. Malloy is one of the neatest people I know." Danny was worked up over the mere thought of someone hurting his favorite teacher. "Damn, now I wish she'd never taken that trip."

"And we can't do a damn thing to help her—"

"—except be there for her." Danny thumped the desk as if that helped cement his promise.

Chapter Nine

Sarah loved the area around Princeton. Students walked the campus and visited the same shops she did. The home she rented suited her with its small yard and wide trees. She and that house had been through hurricane conditions and fierce blizzards. The summer heat didn't sap her strength. The spring revived her, and the arrival of a new long semester term in the autumn left her excited. Her house remained uncluttered even though her office appeared so. In reality, her office was so small that adding a pound of paper to any of the working spaces made the place seem disordered.

Mid-June gave hints of coming warmer weather. Enough that Sarah seldom wore a sweater to the university in the mornings unless she had meetings to attend in rooms that she knew were well air-conditioned. She had three classes Monday, Wednesday and Friday. And two on Tuesday and Thursday. Otherwise, she was in her office, available to students at any time.

After one particularly warm day filled with a department meeting, three classes and seven student conferences, Sarah returned home and flopped into her easy chair. She needed to pull weeds from the small flowerbed in the back yard and check that her oil and air pressure were still good on her 1948 MG. Thankfully, she wasn't one of those persons who filled their garages with boxes and storage shelves, reducing the space for her two cars. Her SUV fit nicely in one side of the wide garage while her little 1948 MG roadster fit in the space left. Sarah loved driving the roadster, but when winter approached, the little car would sit snug in the heated garage until spring. Until then she'd enjoy driving with the top down and wind in her hair.

She had a list of a dozen things to do that afternoon, but fatigue hit her hard. She sat slumped in her chair, staring out the back door with its generous amount of glass. How different that scene from what she saw on break while in Australia. How different from the beach and small house she'd shared with Reagan.

Thoughts of him brought up a sigh. She missed him, even as brief as their liaison had been. Something happened to her heart that weekend. She thought she knew Reagan as well as anyone by the time he boarded his plane, but she had no idea how *his* heart felt. She tucked her legs underneath her and pulled a light lap quilt over her. Her head rested against the tall side of the wingback chair, one hand rubbing the heart-shaped earrings she always wore. The pair Reagan gave her that weekend. Her hand covered her mouth, the better to stifle a possible sob, at the loss of the lovely necklace. How her heart broke over that.

Life seemed so normal at home, in her office with Danny and Bridget and in her classroom. Yet it wasn't normal at all. A very large portion of Sarah's heart left with Reagan the day he flew away for parts unknown. Wherever he worked, there her heart resided.

———

Shortly after Sarah sat at home grieving for the lost necklace and lost love, she noticed the picture on the far wall in her classroom. Thirty Conley prints hung around the room. Each summer she asked Danny and a few of his friends to rearrange the photos. After a while, she was so used to them that she sometimes forgot to really *look* at them.

For some reason that day, she moved to the far corner to counsel a student on her point of view for an essay she was writing. When Sarah stood up from kneeling next to the girl, she was face-to-face with a Conley photo that immediately took on new meaning. The photo showed the corner of a terrace with the weather-beaten railing, a table and the over-sized lounge chair where they had made love several times. In the distance beyond the dunes lay the sparkling waters of the Beagle Gulf that led to the Indian Ocean.

In her mind, Sarah filled in the rest of the picture. To the right, double doors leading to Reagan's bedroom. Behind her, the stairs leading down to the beach.

Her breath caught in a little sob, and she fought to control the tears that sprang immediately to her eyes. God, it was the bungalow in Darwin where she and Reagan spent the week-end. She had been so loved in that house that it became like a second home for her, more real to her than the cozy little home she lived in right here in New Jersey. Pulling herself together, Sarah moved back to the front of the room and continued to help students.

But as soon as the class ended, she asked Danny to remove the picture and take it to her office. There were numerous other prints there to choose from, and she asked him to replace the bungalow photo with another selection. Thanking her assistant as she took the large print from him, she immediately forgot his presence. Sarah sat down in her overstuffed high-backed chair and held the print before her. She lost herself in memories of Reagan and all they did that weekend.

Later she found a crumpled note written back and forth between Danny and Bridget. Danny had missed the trashcan when he apparently tossed it there.

Danny's scribble: Doc looks both sad and happy. Look how she runs her hand over that print.

Bridget's fastidious writing: Did you notice how she acted in class when she stood up and saw that photo? I think that place means a great deal to her.

Danny: She's miles away right now.

Bridget: Yeah, so is he, I guess. Don't take a rocket scientist to know she's in love with that place and that man.

Danny: Yep

Sarah frowned first then let her lips lift in a soft smile. She'd have to be on guard. Those two made good detectives. Of course, she didn't hide her feelings when in the office. She smoothed out the note and put it in her drawer. Later when her T.A.s weren't around, she'd stick it in the back of the photo's frame.

———

Love hurts—Sarah knew it, and now her teaching assistants knew it too. That photo that Danny took down and brought to Sarah's office now hung in a place on the wall where other Conley photo prints hung.

If there's ever a shrine to Reagan Conley prints, Sarah mused, it's here. But she enjoyed seeing the shots so didn't care what others thought.

When a spare moment gave her rest, she often touched the eleven by eight photo of him in a frame on her desk.

"That one's been here since we came," Bridget said one day. "I never knew photographers allowed others to take pictures of them."

"Actually, it's the only one outside his publisher's office. One of his Sherpas snapped the photo then wondered if he'd get in trouble, so he sent it to Reagan's publisher with all rights going to Mr. Nome. My agent and Mr. Nome are friends, so she asked if I could have a copy under penalty of a huge fine if I ever sent it out into the world. I promised, and here it is, safe in my office where no one but us three know the truth." She gave them a pointed stare complete with raised eyebrow, a signal that knowledge of the photo would not come from them.

"Good by me," Danny said as he slapped a hand over his heart. "I'm not about to spill the beans on this secret. Too much trouble to get out of." He gave Sarah a sappy grin.

"If I didn't trust you two, I'd have never told you the story," Sarah assured them. "Does make me feel a bit sneaky about having it. Or at least it used to. I mentioned that photo to him when we talked. So he's aware though he wasn't too happy about it. However, I am delighted." She giggled, something the two had never heard her do.

———

It was the middle of June; the fifteenth to be exact, two days after Sarah discovered the print of the bungalow, when she returned to her office after class to find Bridget signing for a package.

"Who got the package?" She tossed her papers on the desk, opened the drawer and slid her purse in.

"It's addressed to you, Dr. Malloy. It has a funny stamp on

it." Bridget handed it over, pointing to the stamp. "Poor package looks like it's been dragged through Hell." She also pointed out various stains and two frayed corners. "Looks pretty ratty to me, but the wrapping is still intact. Whoever wrapped that did a bang-up job."

Sarah sat down and laid the box on top of her desk. "The handwriting's not familiar."

"No return address either. Just your name and the university's address. Pretty sketchy if you ask me," Bridget commented.

"What's sketchy?" Danny came through the door, tossed his backpack in his desk chair and joined Sarah and Bridget at her desk. "What's that? Where'd it come from? Who's it for?"

"Don't know. Came from some place foreign," Bridget pointed to the stamp, "and it's for Doc."

"Okay then. What are we waiting for? Open it, Doc," he encouraged as he propped a hip on the corner of her desk. "I'm dying of curiosity here." Punching Dr. Malloy lightly on the shoulder, Danny urged her to open the silly thing instead of all three of them sitting there in suspense.

"It's probably a story from one of my students. I get them now and then. Especially when they get one published. They like to brag."

While they laughed over that comment, Sarah carefully removed the multiple layers of rough brown wrapping paper and uncovered two pieces of heavy cardboard.

"Boy, whatever it is, someone didn't want it to be damaged!" Danny commented as he took the heavy paper and folded it.

Sarah smiled over her shoulder at him as she removed the top piece of cardboard but sucked in her breath so quickly she choked. Lying in her lap was a photo in color of *herself*!

Over her shoulder, she heard Danny whisper "Awesome"

93

as well as Bridget's "Oh, Dr. Malloy" that came in a whispered tender voice.

Sarah hesitantly reached out to the picture. Touching it would make it real. It was a picture of Sarah sitting in the middle of Reagan's bed on that Sunday morning. She sat cross-legged with a cup of coffee in her hand. Her head was bent forward as she read the newspaper scattered across the sheets. The bed was unmade. She sat there as comfortable as can be in an open shirt and nothing else. Of course, one couldn't see anything personal, but it was obvious she wore nothing under the shirt. That beautiful necklace lay on her chest.

She ran her finger down the long chair and sighed. "I was so upset that last day. He was leaving near noon, and we gathered up my things. But we couldn't find that necklace. I'd laid it quite carefully on the night table next to the bed. But it was gone. We turned that little house upside down but never found it. I cried when we couldn't find it. I have the earrings that I wear all the time. But that necklace was so..." She stopped when words failed.

"Special huh?" Danny attempted to finish her sentence.

"More than special," Bridget amended.

"I mourn its loss." Sarah said as she propped the photo up against a stack of books. It had touched every part of their bodies before the weekend ended so carried a lifetime's worth of memories in its gold, silver and black.

Sarah blushed a little when she realized Danny and Bridget saw the photo that was pretty private, at least to her.

"That's beautiful," said Bridget reverently. Danny agreed with a discreet nod.

"You ought to buy a lovely frame for that and put it here on your desk, Dr. Malloy. It's a stunning photo." Bridget suggested. Ever the bolder of the two, Bridget commented as she returned to the work interrupted by the delivery, "You know, some might consider that a racy photo. But he makes it look like..." she searched for a second as Sarah watched her. "... like reading the Sunday newspaper. Neither one of us will ever ask if Reagan Conley took that photo. I think we know the answer to that one on our own. We know how to keep our mouths shut, and this is definitely one of those times." She snagged Danny's shirtsleeve and jerked her head toward the door.

"I'm off to find a Coke and some cookies, Doc. Want something?" Danny offered a way for the two of them to leave Dr. Malloy alone for a little bit.

"Uh, yes please. Chocolate chip cookies if you can find them." She turned back to the photo and gave them no further thought. She ran her hand over the print. Then she glanced at the wrapping paper. There was no return address. But as she thought of Reagan, she remembered that his publicist always knew where he was and could get a letter to him anytime, anywhere.

Sarah laid the photo on its cardboard down on her desk, opened a drawer and removed a pair of scissors. Working carefully, she cut out the mailing stamp. It was a foreign country, and she didn't recognize the words.

Where in the world are you, Reagan, she wondered as she laid the stamp aside then refolded the rest of the brown paper and stuffed it into the trashcan.

She turned to remove the two pieces of cardboard that had protected the photograph on its journey from wherever in the world it had come. As she slid the bottom piece of board out from under the picture, it lifted and turned over. There on the back of the photo was something she almost missed. Reagan had written her a letter. In bold sprawling writing, he wrote:

June 2015

Good morning, my darling,
*   I am in the foothills of the Himalayan Mountains. It's cold as a witch's tits in winter. When I see this photo of you though, I feel warm again...warm because of the sun and sand. Mainly I feel warm because of you...your skin, the way it feels. Your eyes, the way they burn into me when you look at me. Remember that morning? What a lovely sight you made, sitting in the middle of my bed. That's one of the things I remember about that weekend. I remember everything.*

Love, Reagan

Sarah cried before she even finished reading the short message. Everything she wanted was out there somewhere in the world with that man. How she wanted him. She wanted him here right now with her. He wasn't here of course, but he sent a lovely present to help her remember. Oh, yes. She remembered...everything.

Sarah sat down the very afternoon she received Reagan's gift and began writing. She wrote about everything, told him serious things and funny things. She wrote about the classes she was teaching, the weather, and her trip home without him. The only thing she didn't tell him that day was how much she loved him. She did tell him that she missed him though. Addressing the envelope to Reagan Conley in care of his publicist, she put a stamp on it and dropped it in the campus mailbox on her way home. She had a purpose now. She would write to Reagan every week.

Taking Bridget's suggestion, Dr. Malloy bought a beautiful frame, copied the letter on the back of the photo on to her computer then placed the picture on her desk. She wondered what Bridget and Danny would say to her having a photo of herself on her own desk.

"Wow! Doc, that's looks great." Bridget spotted the photo first where Sarah tucked it around a pile of books, discrete but visible. "I'm happy you have things like that to remind you of that time with him since you don't have the necklace anymore."

Beyond that, the two never said another word, but she caught them grinning now and then when they caught her touching Reagan's photo.

———

The Fourth of July came and went. Sarah wrote her letters to Reagan, and the second summer semester began. Many of Sarah's former students stopped by her office for her advice on various things and to visit. They often spoke of the photos hanging in her classroom or debated the lyrics of the music she played. As if by some unspoken law, however, no one said anything about the photo of a woman sitting half-naked in bed reading a newspaper. There had to be some connection between that photo and the very informal one of Reagan Conley just to the front of hers.

On the fifteenth of July, Sarah sat in her office working on essays while Danny entered grades on the computer. Bridget had come by the office looking for a quiet place to work.

"Mind if I hang out here, Doc? I have a physics assignment due, and I can't think anywhere else."

"Certainly. Danny's entering grades, and I'm grading papers so it's quiet as a tomb."

Bridget settled, nodded to Danny, and soon the three were in their own world, doing their own thing.

The windows were opened, and a warm breeze played with the papers each one worked with. But the office wasn't too warm, and it was pleasant. When someone knocked on the office door, Sarah was knee-deep in an essay and didn't even notice, so Danny rolled his chair over and opened the door.

"Delivery."

"Sure thing."

"Sign here."

Danny closed the door and rolled his chair over to Sarah's desk. On the way, he reached out and slapped Bridget's arm. Uttering a little screech and demanding to know why he hit her, Bridget quickly shut her mouth when she saw what Danny had in his hand.

"Dr. Malloy?"

Sarah was so into the essay she read that she didn't hear him at first.

"Dr. Malloy...a package came for you." Danny spoke louder as he slid the large package between her and the essay. Sarah jumped back a little, startled by the unexpected intrusion.

"What? What's this, Danny?" And then she closed her mouth as fast as Bridget had. There on her desk was another package wrapped in the same brown paper and carrying another mailing stamp from a different foreign country.

"A foreign stamp. No return address," Bridget stated the obvious.

"But the handwriting is the same," Sarah said quietly. Daring to glance at the two students who had pulled up close to her, Sarah reached for the package with trembling hands. Carefully unwrapping the whole affair, she let the paper fall to the floor beside her desk. A thick piece of cardboard lay on top and bottom. Sandwiched between was what? Sarah took a deep breath and slid the top board aside.

"Oh my God!" She had no idea which one of them uttered that.

It was a study in shadow and light. Pale silver bluish light reflected off the side of a nude woman standing under some sort of shower mounted on a wall outside. The deep shades of night obscured almost everything including most of the woman. Moonlight outlined her body from the extended fingers of her raised left arm, down past her face hidden behind her arm, down past her ribs and breast that peeked out provocatively, down her left hip on past her thigh, bent knee and foot that rested on its tiptoes. All else was in varying shades of black and gray. It was breathtaking in simplicity, implication and grace.

This time Sarah couldn't hold back the tears, nor did she try to hide them. She vividly recalled the night Reagan took this shot, but more importantly, she remembered the loving that followed right there in that shower. She never quite knew when the kids left the office that afternoon. She vaguely felt Danny's hand resting gently on her shoulder for a second or two. Long after they left, she sat, studying every inch of the print.

Sarah was afraid to turn the photograph over.

What if he didn't write something on the back?

Finally, she couldn't stand the self-torture any longer. Turning the print over, she breathed a sigh of relief.

July 2015

My darling,

Received two of your letters today. What a delightful surprise! When I read your words, I can see you as you walk across campus or work with one of your students. Don't talk to me about hot, Sarah, I'm in the deserts of Israel. Now this is hot! What do you think of the Night Goddess? That's how I think of you when the temperature at night here is the same as the day. You're cool and seductive, mysterious and wanton.

You're every man's dream. That's when I see you the most...in my dreams. Remember what we did after I took this shot? I felt so powerful there with you because you let me have the power to make you a woman in all ways. I remember that night. In this long journey that I am on, I remember everything.

Love, Reagan

Sarah's heart already held more love than she thought she could possess. Where was that man when she needed him so badly that her insides hurt? It was all she could do not to climax right here in the chair in her very own office! She ran her fingers over Reagan's words then picked up the print and kissed where his hand had lain. After cutting out the mailing stamp and laying it with the print, she took out pen and paper and began her letter that week.

The next day, Sarah added another framed picture to the two already standing on her desk. Students still came by, and they noticed.

"We're watching a romance," one girl whispered to another in Sarah's class several days later. The young woman had spent an hour with Sarah working on an essay. She apparently saw the photos. Those along with the ones in the office probably led to that comment.

While Sarah couldn't say a romance blossomed, she knew she loved Reagan Conley desperately. How he felt she couldn't say. If she had just asked Danny or Bridget they would have said, "Doc, you're the one who needs to be told things...like this is right or this isn't worth a shit. Let me tell you, the man loves you. Hands down. No question about it."

By the middle of August, Sarah and her teaching assistants gave up the great outdoors of open windows and hot summer breezes and opted instead for good old air conditioning. Sarah seemed to have a lot of visitors on that August fifteenth. She got a little annoyed when the sixth group of students *dropped by* for a chat. She wasn't getting any of her work done with all these interruptions.

With Bridget and Danny plus three former students who came by to visit about fall classes they wanted to take, it was pretty crowded in her corner office. When someone knocked at the door, a silence sudden and total fell over the place and caused Sarah to shiver.

This is positively spooky, she thought. What in the world was the matter with this bunch?

Bridget answered the door, accepted the familiar package then turned to Sarah.

It dawned on her at that point just why all these kids were here. Each one was a favorite of hers, and each one was familiar with how much she liked Reagan's work. Now she figured each one was also familiar with just who might be sending these packages and just who was responsible for the growing collection of photographs on her desk. Rather than say something that would hurt their feelings, she just gave them all one of *those* looks, shook her head, and accepted the item.

"That stamp looks familiar, Doc. Russia maybe?" Danny almost had his nose on top of the stamp.

"Russia definitely," one of the other students said. "My uncle travels there and sends letters back now and then so we'll have something really cool."

Russia! Oh Lord, what is Reagan doing in Russia or anywhere near there? There is fighting going on in that part of the world.

His publicist in New York never mentioned any risks, but Sarah suspected danger generally found Reagan.

As she unwrapped the heavy brown paper, she placed the package on her desk so the people behind her could see over her shoulder. This time when she uncovered the picture, her eyes went all soft, and she smiled one of those sneaky smiles.

This wasn't a picture of her; it was a picture of Reagan. But if you didn't *know* who the man was, you wouldn't be able to tell. It was a rather good photo if she did say so.

I wonder what Reagan thought when he got his prints developed and found *this* one. He didn't know it was on there. But I knew.

A chuckle escaped her, another one of those seldom-heard affirmations of high humor. She remembered it well. That last Sunday night she fell asleep quickly in Reagan's embrace. Later in the night, something woke her. He wasn't next to her. He lay at the far edge of the bed facing the doors and the moonlight. Sarah went to the bathroom then walked to the doors to admire the view outside. When she turned around, the uniqueness of the setting caught her attention. She had taken only one other photograph of Reagan earlier in the evening, another one he didn't know about and probably choked over when he finally saw it. Moving quietly to the nightstand, she took up the camera then moved back near the door. She moved until she found the picture she wanted. Snapping the lens, she returned the camera to its original place then got back in bed. When she lay down, Sarah remembered that Reagan rolled over to her side and threw an arm around her ribs. Curling into the curve of his body, she had fallen back to sleep.

Now she saw the final product and couldn't help but admire her own work. Slashes of moonlight lay across the carpet. The light cut across a man's arm hanging off a bed where he lay sleeping on his stomach. A sheet draped over his hip and one leg lay curled on top. Light and shadows fell over the man's face, lacing it with moonlight that disguised him. All else in the room was bathed in darkness. Only Sarah knew who the man was and who took the picture.

Sarah admired the photo and longed to touch the image of Reagan but waited patiently for the students to do something. No one said a word. Nothing. She looked over her shoulder to see five pair of eyes scrutinizing the work. As if waking up from a dream induced by that very picture, each gaze rose to meet hers.

"Your work?" one student asked. Sarah just nodded.

"Wish I could take a photo as good as that," sighed one student as she rose to leave. Sarah bid them goodbye but almost lost her composure when one of the other girls leaving the office commented, "*Anyone* can take a good picture if the subject looks as good as him." Though whispered, Sarah had tuned into their parting comments, curiosity blazing.

Bridget shooed Danny out the door and yelled, "Night, Doc!"

Oh, Reagan, she thought. What you're doing to my students and me! It's a sin...God love you!

With that thought in mind, she clipped the mailing stamp off the brown paper, which she threw away then flipped the print over. There was his letter, written in a hurry evidently. She hoped nothing was wrong.

August 2015

My sneaky darling,

I taught you well, I see. And just when did you take this little jewel? I'll have to watch you around the cameras and me from now on. No really, Sarah, it's a great picture... wonderful composition and a very effective use of light and dark. Reminds me of another picture I saw with a model in shadows and light. My journey has led me to Russia...I can't say where exactly. You'll see the photos soon in major magazines, I'm sure. While I huddle here in the cold, I remember how warm you feel in my arms. Sometimes those memories of holding you are all that get me through these damn cold nights. With my fingers numb and cracking, I'm wondering if this journey was really necessary! Remember the house where we made love? I remember everything.

Love, Reagan

Sarah turned the print back over and sat for a while just looking at it. She studied the lines and how the shape of the human body is such a glorious thing. Unlike the dark study of her sitting in the frame already on her desk, she cherished this photo because Reagan had sent her a picture of himself. Granted his face wasn't clear, but *she* knew it was him, and that's what counted. Sarah ran her finger down the line of Reagan's body from his head past the hip across the sheet-draped buttocks to the long leg lying there in a brilliant patch of moonlight. She traced the arch of his shoulder and the curve of his neck where her head fit so perfectly, and he smelled so good. Getting up and locking her door, Sarah returned to her chair and allowed her daydreams to become erotic.

Oh, Reagan, what a letter I have to write this time, she giggled. Maybe I'll include my erotic dreams. How wicked of me. How perfect.

Chapter Ten

The fall semester of school began with meetings and budget concerns. Dr. Malloy's classes filled her days, and the writing that resulted from student assignments filled her nights. But when she laid the work aside and fell into bed exhausted, it was Reagan she dreamed about. Her letters to him grew each week. She told him all her concerns and adventures. Sarah wasn't even sure he was getting all of the novels she wrote, but she hoped so. There had never been any promises between them, but she felt closer to Reagan Conley than any other human on earth.

"Anything on my schedule this afternoon, Bridget, other than what I've written here?" Sarah went over her daily calendar every morning and again just before she left the office.

"Nothing I know of, Doc."

"Dr. Malloy, a student came by the other day and asked for time to visit with you, and I forgot to leave a note for you. For your calendar. Sorry." Danny wheeled around in his chair and held out a note. "I left it on my desk and laid something on it. I think the appointment is for this afternoon."

"Way to go, genius," Bridget chided. "I think Doc wanted to run some errands."

"Not a big deal, Bridget. Leave him alone," Sarah chided the girl as she accepted the note. "Let's see. Thomas Penning. The name sounds familiar. Why is that?" She sat back in her chair, propped an elbow on the armrest and closed her eyes. "Penning. Penning. That rings bells."

"Maybe he's a former student. Or someone in one of your special classes." Danny ticked off several places where she might have heard the name.

"That evening class! That's it. Tom Penning." She shook her head. "Boy, he was a handful."

Sarah taught one evening class a semester for students who had trouble handling larger class settings. Often these were students with a high degree of Attention Deficit Disorder or sometimes students with hearing impairment. Though they wanted to attend her regular class, the movement, fast conversation, and noise level put them off. So the department granted Sarah permission to host ten students a semester in her classroom in the evenings twice a week for two hours each session.

"Those can be pretty challenging classes, you've told us." Bridget laid aside her papers and turned her chair to face Danny and Sarah. "You said you weren't comfortable a few times."

"There have been a few times when I wished one of you were in the room with me. But, of course, that's not what the department agreed to. I think those young people are a challenge simply because their entire life has been such. My class is perhaps as close as some have gotten to what they term a *normal* class. But they all admit the small number and quieter setting help them learn better."

"Can they write like you ask them to?" Danny had returned to his desk but asked that over his shoulder.

"To my delight, yes, they can. It seems, as one student told me, they can often put down on paper what they want me to know better than trying to find verbal words to use. Maybe it's because too they have more time to find those words that they write and aren't rushed."

"Well, for whatever reason, this Thomas Penning wants to visit with you."

"I'm going to continue grading, Danny, but let me know when he shows up."

"Can do."

Late that afternoon, Bridget was gone, and Danny was prepared to leave. Thomas Penning had yet to show up.

"How much longer will you be here, Doc?" He gathered his backpack and tossed paper in the trash can.

"Another hour at least. If Mr. Penning shows up, he'll have to leave when I do. My neighbor is picking me up at five. I put my MG in the garage to have its annual inspection. Sophie is taking me there then following me home."

"Why don't you set your cell phone alarm for oh say, four-fifty, then you won't get lost in those essays and realize it's dark outside and you have to scramble to get to that ride."

"Good idea. It will also be a signal to this Penning that it's time to leave."

"Night, Doc."

"Night, Danny."

Pulling out her cell phone, Sarah set her alarm so it would go off at four-fifty. Then she returned to her papers.

Sometime later, a firm knock rattled her office door. Glancing at the cell that laid on her desk, she saw it was already four-fifteen. She left her desk and opened the door to see a young man standing there, backpack over one shoulder, coffee cup in hand.

"Can I help you?" She wasn't letting a stranger into the

office unless it was Penning. The guy looked familiar, but he had that general *student* look to him so that didn't help.

"I'm Thomas Penning. I have an appointment with you. I was supposed to be here at four, but that damn barista at the coffee shop doesn't like me, so she did several orders ahead of me before getting to mine."

"We have about a half hour before I have to leave. You can come in, and I'll try to help you if I can." Sarah stood back and pulled the door wide open, allowing him to enter. However, she left the door open and flipped on the bright overhead light. "Take that chair." Once Penning was seated with his coffee cup on a pile of essays on Danny's desk and the backpack on the floor, Sarah turned her chair so she could face him and see the open door at the same time.

"How do we know each other, Mr. Penning? Have you taken one of my classes or anticipate taking one?"

"I took your evening class earlier this year."

"Summer or winter semester?"

"Winter. And it was a damn cold winter too. That was the only night class I had, and by the time we left class and I walked to my apartment, I was about frozen every time."

"I'm sorry you suffered so much discomfort. I hope the class helped with your creative writing."

"Oh, it did. Thank you. I believe you were the motivating force in awakening my writing talents." Penning sat forward, not as an excited student but more as someone...

Sarah couldn't find a word that fit how he looked at her. As if he expected her to be more than she offered. Shaking her head at such a silly notion, she continued the conversation, hoping to discover why he wanted to meet.

"Your visit here today is because?"

"I am working on a major novel, creating a masterpiece that several publishers are already interested in. They've read the summary and have asked for a draft by next May. I'm hoping you'll be my sounding board and advisor for the project."

Not sure how to answer—his proposal wasn't like anything she'd ever been offered—she sat back and focused on him.

Once he stated his intentions, he too sat back in Danny's chair, crossed an ankle over a knee and sipped his coffee, apparently not in a hurry for her answer. Rather than look around her office, he focused as steadily on her as she did on him. To the point that she almost squirmed.

"Just so I understand, you want me to sort of...edit...your first draft?"

"I suppose you could say that. I created my characters, but sometimes have difficulty with where they lead me as far as their behavior."

To most that would sound odd at the very least and delusional at the extreme, but Sarah was a writer and worked with budding writers so understood that while you create characters in your mind, at times when you write a scene a particular character veers away from what you had in mind. Trying to bring that personality back to what the author planned sometimes produced self-inflicted stress.

"You need a beta reader to see if your characters are wandering away from the story line, is that it?"

"I suppose."

"I am flattered, Mr. Penning. I am a full time working professor with obligations to my current students. I can find some time to assist you but can't be at your beck and call for editing or advice at the drop of a hat." She had to make it clear that she would not obligate herself to his every whim and demand of her time.

"You help students all the time, Sarah."

At Sarah's startled expression, he amended quickly. "I

meant to say Dr. Malloy. I can't imagine how that slipped out."

While his words apologized, his sly glance indicated he relished her reaction.

Am I reading too much into this man's words and actions? He wants help I can provide though maybe not as often as he'd like.

"True, I help others, but I focus on helping those in my current classes. I carry a full load each day and work in the office on their essays as well as mentor them. You have a head start on those currently in my classes. You've taken the class in peace and quiet which I have to admit isn't always found in any of my classes." She held out a hand palm up in an attempt to help him understand that he was a former student, and she owed her time and skills to those now with her. "Surely someone at your prospective publisher can offer more valid advice than me."

"No!" Penning almost shouted. Immediately he calmed. "Sorry. I've asked for advice from the publisher. Based on my college transcript they suggested I consult you on this work in progress."

"Oh, I see." Sarah always tried to help her students, but this man's request meant she'd be more involved than time permitted. Or she wanted to be.

"Let me think on your request, Mr. Penning—"

"Thomas or just Tom as you called me in class, please." His interruption exuded sincerity.

"Okay, Tom. I have a half hour free time for consultation in..." She turned to her desk calendar. "Next week. Next Monday at 4:30." She held out her hands, palms up, and shrugged. "That's the best I can do."

Rather than answer Sarah, Tom jumped to an entirely new topic.

"Is that the photographer you're so crazy about? What's

his name? Ronald? Raymond?" Penning sat forward in his chair, one hand clinched, the coffee cup in danger of being crumpled. A slight sneer slipped across his lips. His gaze hardened.

"Reagan Conley. Yes, I like his photos along with several other professionals. As well as several musicians and artists. I use them as starting points for my students' writings." She sat a little straighter. "As you well know."

"Yes. Yes. I remember. I remember it all."

Odd how him saying that echoes Reagan's words but with a totally different meaning, she realized.

"You're friends?"

"I had the pleasure of meeting him early in the summer."

"I see." Tom settled back in his chair, snapped the cup to his mouth, finished off the coffee then left it sitting on the desk.

The cell phone alarm went off just then. Sarah couldn't honestly say she wasn't pleased to have a designated ending to this meeting. She vowed though not to have a meeting alone with Tom Penning again though. Bridget or better yet, Danny would be present even if she had to bribe them with a pizza or some cold hard cash.

"That's the timer I set earlier this afternoon. I have an errand to run and must leave now." She stood and clasped her hands together in front of her. "I'll see you next Monday then around this same time. I must remind you that I shut up the office at five, so please be on time."

He gathered his pack, stood, and took a step closer to Sarah.

She held her ground.

"I'll be here. On time." Without another word, he marched out of the office, his posture being one who dismissed her rather than her dismissing him. As if it were his meeting rather than hers.

With time running out, Sarah grabbed her light sweater, her own book bag and purse. She stepped into the hall, looking for anyone who might still be around. From the office down the hall, she spotted Dr. Jean Cramer doing the same thing—locking her office door.

"Wait up, Jean, and we'll walk together."

The woman waved to show she heard. Sarah walked quickly to her side and out to her neighbor's waiting car. Sophie invited her over for a hot meal and good wine. Sarah accepted and in the process of a lovely evening, she totally forgot her instinctive discomfort during the meeting with Tom Penning.

———

The following Monday came and went without Tom Penning showing up. Danny volunteered to hang around until she left the office, which she promised faithfully would be at five.

"No show, huh." Danny gathered his things and a jacket. A cold front had pushed through the night before and left a chill on Monday morning that warmed up by mid-afternoon.

"I'm not sure how reliable Mr. Penning is, to be honest. I checked my records for that class he attended. He managed to miss several classes. He passed but not with high marks, though his writing is good. Dynamic in a way. Almost frenetic."

"Oh, before we leave, I found this under the door while you waited. I glanced at it because it had no name on it. Not even an envelope. From a student I guess, but whoever it was didn't leave a name." He handed over the note and opened the door but waited while Sarah read the note.

Puzzled by it, she read it aloud. "You're beautiful and smart. Too smart to hook up with a loser who will leave you. Keep teaching, and forget those old guys." She held the note up, her mouth twisted to one side, her brows pulled down. "Does this make any sense to you?"

"Nope. Sounds like a nut job to me." He took a step into the hall. "Time to go, Doc. I'll walk you to your car."

"No need. I'll be fine."

"No worries, Doc. I'm going in that direction anyway." He pulled the door shut and waited as she locked it. Together they went downstairs and out into a late evening with the sun already behind the stately buildings. Her car was in the faculty parking lot and that lay in deep shadows.

Danny turned and waved but stopped when he heard Sarah's explanation.

"Damn! I've got a flat tire. And I just got all the tires checked out." She bent over to run a hand over the side of the tire. But she jerked it back quickly and stuck her finger in her mouth. "Something's sticking out."

"Let me see." Danny laid his things aside and went down on one knee. Carefully he ran his hand over the flat. He stopped and used his fingers to inspect something. "Feels like a nail, Doc."

"A nail? Where would I pick up something like that?"

"Don't know but let's get it changed so you can get home."

By the time Danny changed the tire, fit the flat back into its place on the rear of the little roadster the sun had set, and the lot was not only dark but almost empty.

"I can't thank you enough," Sarah told him as he gathered his things. A stiff breeze had blown up while he worked. His dorm was on the other side of the large campus. "The least I can do is give you a lift home. Hop in."

The canvas roof was up so while Sarah had no trouble sliding into the small car Danny had to maneuver his larger body in carefully. A good laugh helped ease the frustration of a flat tire.

"Get that tire fixed tomorrow, Doc. You never can tell when that might happen again."

"Will do, but I doubt there'll be any more trouble."

———

"Doc, there's a package for you." Bridget walked over to Sarah's desk with a small box in her hand.

"Oh?" Sarah glanced at her calendar. The date was nowhere around the middle of the month so she doubted it would be from Reagan, but who?

"Well, let's see what it is? What about a return address?"

"None. In fact, I don't see a stamp or postal mark either." She gave it to Sarah but stood by.

"Odd. Hand delivered?"

"Sitting on the main desk downstairs. The receptionist turned to a cabinet for about thirty seconds, she said, and when she turned back, there it was. Of course, a lot of students pass through about this time of day so any one of them could have left it there without being noticed."

"Curiouser and curiouser," Sarah said as she undid the tape. "A secret admirer perhaps." She grinned, thinking that was a good joke. However, when the paper came off and she opened the box, she had her doubts.

"Is that a heart?" Bridget took a step closer and almost put her nose into the box. "That's sick."

"I don't think it's real, Bridget. Look." Bolder than even her brave teaching assistant, Sarah ran a fingertip around the edge of what looked like a bloodied small heart. "It's clay and that—" she lifted a finger to smell the liquid, "—is ketchup."

"Hey look, Doc. There's a note tucked into the top of the box." Bridget used a fingernail to slide the paper out onto Sarah's desk. "What's it say?" She could see the note perfectly well but had been with Dr. Malloy long enough not to step on her authority.

"I'd give you my heart—bloodied and bruised—if you wanted it." Sarah read the note then sat back. "I'm not sure what to make of this."

"Admit it, Doc. This is just plain creepy."

"I agree. But it's not cruel. Better than a real heart." Sarah slid the top back on the box but left the note lying on her desk. "And our fingerprints are now all over the box and paper. And I touched the clay heart."

"What are you thinking, Doc?" Bridget stretched out her arm, grabbed her chair and pulled it over beside Sarah.

"I think I need to notify the campus police. This may be a perfectly harmless show of affection though it's disturbing. Or it could be a sign of someone with a sick mind."

"Yeah, and an obsession for you." Bridget almost reached out to touch the box but quickly drew back her hand. "Or someone out to make you miserable."

"True. I refuse to be miserable over this. But I am taking precautions. Just in case. Let me make a phone call." Her mind set on a plan, she reached for the desk phone and contacted the campus police.

———

"One of our officers is downstairs now checking the security tape. You got it today so whoever left it will show up."

"I don't think so, Sergeant," said an officer coming in the door.

"How's that, Dickens?"

"There were a number of students in and out. It's chilly outside today with a stiff breeze. Most of them are wearing hoodies pulled up. I can see few faces. They're in a hurry, and most are in groups. And as those groups pass the front desk, a few of the kids jostled each other so it's hard to tell if someone laid something on the reception desk or not. Three groups passed through before the box showed up. In between those groups were enough passing to prevent seeing the actual desk. The receptionist was at the file cabinet, the computer and on the phone or helping someone most of the time rather than sitting with a view of the front of the desk."

"Okay. So that's a dead end," Sergeant Tremont said. "Perhaps we can get some information from the box or note. Or maybe from the paper that wrapped up the box." He held out a gloved hand and accepted the three items.

"I took a cell photo of both the box and note, Sergeant. If that's all right."

"Of course, Dr. Malloy. No harm in that. You'd already touched these. Your T. A. had touched the box and paper. We expect to find your prints on them. Maybe the receptionist's prints as well."

The box didn't bother Sarah as much as it did Bridget. The girl squirmed and seemed about to speak but held her tongue.

"Any enemies, Dr. Malloy?"

"Me?" Sarah knew her eyes grew wide, and her mouth fell open in shock.

"Her?" Bridget shouted that and jumped up. "You have to be kidding. She's the kindest, most generous person you'd ever find. Everyone loves her. Even that damn bloody heart attests to that."

"Easy, Bridget. Your Irish temper is showing," Sarah teased in an effort to calm the fiery redhead.

"Enemies, my foot!" Bridget snorted before returning to her chair.

"We can look at this two ways. One is someone with some funny ideas of love. Or it's someone who has a grudge against you. Or wants something you're not giving. Any way you look at it, we'll get these tested and see what kind of information prints can give us." Tremont and Dickens moved to the door. "Has anyone been hassling you?"

"Hassling? Good lord no. I have students adamant about their assignments and grades but nothing out of the ordinary."

"Keep us posted if anything changes. And Doc, you might have someone with you while on campus. Just to be on the safe side."

"Is that necessary?"

"Maybe not. This might be a one-off as they say. But then again it could be the beginning of something unpleasant."

Both officers nodded as they left.

"What would Mr. Conley say if he knew about this?" Bridget still sat but held her hands clasped rather tightly in her lap. A worried frown seemed glued to her face.

"We'll never know because he'll never find out." Sarah never told her teaching assistants that she wrote to him each week. She had no plans on telling him about this sick sort of joke. It could be a student with a crush on her, and she didn't want to hurt him. Or even her. Lord knows, people doing these sorts of things in this day and age could be a man *or* a woman.

"The sergeant is right about one thing though, Doc."

"What would that be?"

"You shouldn't be alone while at the university. Danny and I will be here with you from the time you come in until you leave. And like Danny did the other night, one of us will walk you to your car."

"That's really not necessary, Bridget, and you know it."

"It is necessary, and you know it!" Bridget's temper rose a notch.

"Calm down. Both of you or at least one of you is always

here. As for the other night, Danny did walk me to my car and lucky for me he did too."

"How do you mean?"

"I had a flat on the roadster. He changed it, and I gave him a lift to his dorm before heading home."

"See! You need us!"

"It was just a nail, not a knife through the tire."

"That may be, but no one's going to hurt you while we're nearby."

Sarah wanted to rub her forehead and wipe out the headache that pounded there. Bad enough that someone sent her a strange gift but now Bridget acted like a mother hen. Sarah admitted though, maybe for a while she might be more comfortable with one of the kids in the room. Rather than escalate Bridget's vow of protection, Sarah gave in graciously.

"Thank you, Bridget. I will feel better with you and Danny here."

"Damn right, Doc!"

Chapter Eleven

"You're late...by a week." Sarah pointed to a chair, inviting Tom Penning to sit. Danny was filing papers at a large cabinet, so Penning sat in his, the one he used two weeks prior.

"I had reasons for not showing." Penning dropped his book bag and crossed one ankle over the other.

Bridget and Danny kept their backs to him, but Sarah noticed they both used the mirrors each brought in the morning after that heart in a box incident. Now she realized they could remain anonymous, so to speak, but still see her and any visitor in their mirrors. Paranoid maybe but comforting.

"You could have called and let me know."

"You kept on doing what you always do. And then you left at five, like you always do. So my absence really didn't bother you at all."

"I suppose that's one way of looking at the situation." Sarah refused to let the young man fluster her. He was correct. She did continue to grade rather than watch the clock for him to show. Him not showing up didn't bother her at all. The flat tire did but not his absence.

"Still you have a responsibility to honor your obligations or at the very least let the other person know you're not coming."

"Whatever." He tossed off her admonishment without a shred of apparent remorse.

"Now that you're here, how may I help you?"

"Look over these pages. It's a scene that won't do what I want. And your helpers here can take a break. They bother me."

"I'm sorry if they bother you, but they stay. So far, they've not said a word to either of us nor made eye contact with either of us. They have work to do, and I pay them to do it. So they stay."

"Whatever," he commented again. This time he sounded irritated. Without further comment, he pulled out four pages and thrust them at Sarah. "Read these."

No *please*. Being around him all the time must be a trial, Sarah thought as she maintained her bland expression.

"Give me a few minutes to read this, please." So saying, she dropped her gaze to the pages, assured that Danny and Bridget watched him.

She glanced at her clock and noted the time neared five. "I have to leave at five, Tom. But I can offer you some advice about your wayward characters. You might..."

Ten minutes later she stopped. Tom's face remained as red now as it did thirty seconds after she began giving him her thoughts on his writing.

"You're upset." She said it calmly, as a matter of fact, rather than a question. No one needed to point out the fact that he was angry and had been for several minutes. "Your characters seem to have no plan for getting out of this situation. You've written them into a corner. As the author, you have every right to do that, but you must never corner your characters without a scene to follow that brings them out of danger or wherever you put them. It's in the planning, Tom. Think the scene through first before you write, then you can stick your characters in whatever danger you want them in, but you already know how to save them. Life treats us like that sometimes, you know. Pushes us into a corner and we see no way out. Life's not as simple as writing a novel, however. We seldom see the bad situation coming so can't plan ahead. May I suggest you change the things I mentioned and then see if your characters don't come out the other side in better shape?"

"Has life pushed you into a corner with him?" Tom jerked a hand toward Reagan's photo on her desk.

"That's a personal question, and I don't answer those kinds of things with my students. And seldom even with my friends." She turned a cold glare on him. "I suggest we stick to your novel. You said you have a deadline, so we need to get these characters headed in the right direction."

"Whatever." That seemed to be his favorite word when she knew he had a huge vocabulary. The young man was a brilliant learner if a rather solitary learning disabled one.

Sarah stood and gestured toward the door. "I'll set aside the last half hour next Monday for you, Tom." She didn't offer him a choice of day or time. Take it or leave it, was her new motto with him. He was a difficult student when he took her class last winter. He hadn't changed much.

He left without a word, leaving the door open.

When his footsteps receded down the hall, Sarah flopped into her desk chair and blew out a big breath. "Well, that was fun—*not*!"

"I'm ready to sit down. I finished filing ten minutes ago but couldn't take my eyes off that nutter."

"Another Aussie word, huh, Danny." Bridget swiveled her chair around to face them. "That is one weird dude."

"Not any worse than he was in that class last winter. About the same. Maybe a bit more stressed because of this book deal. Nothing unusual for a new writer." Sarah gave Tom Penning the benefit of the doubt no matter what impression he left with Bridget and Danny.

"He could be trouble," Danny commented as he noted the time. "Time to leave, ladies."

"Oh right." Sarah and Bridget gathered their things, and all three headed down the hall after locking up.

"He's not trouble, Danny. Penning, I mean. Just determined," was Sarah's last comment as they parted company in the parking lot where the two students insisted walking her.

"Trouble works on a sliding scale, Doc. Gets big then slides back to small then escalates again. That's all I'm saying." Bridget gave Sarah a friendly pat on the back like someone worldly-wise.

"Duly noted, my friend. Duly noted," Sarah acknowledged.

———

As the month matured, Sarah put a word in the ears of her teaching assistants. No innocent *dropping by* would be tolerated on the fifteenth. She didn't need to explain any further; they both understood. Okay, so there wouldn't be a bunch of kids who came to see the latest Reagan Conley photograph. That's the way she wanted it. Wasn't it?

Oh hell, Sarah didn't know any more. The kids were so supportive of the whole thing that it seemed like a very extended family. Though there were a few students in her classes who weren't particularly enthusiastic about being there, most of the kids seemed to enjoy the class even if they detested the writing. But after reading a few essays aloud, the young writers learned they *could* push the envelope and expand their abilities beyond their limits.

Even Tom Penning didn't bother Sarah. He was annoying. Impertinent. Rude at times and lacked the basic sense of courtesy, but then students like him often did. She had taught that smaller evening class enough times to know that students like Tom needed someone to listen and offer guidance, not someone who forced them to do this or that. Of course, she still had to give grades, but she was scrupulous about keeping the kids informed about their grades. Pass, fail, near fail—none were surprised at the end of the semester.

———

The morning of September fifteenth dawned under overcast skies with the threat of a late season hurricane churning in the Atlantic. Even though the forecast predicted the worst of the weather would miss the New Jersey area, the day was still heavy and humid, miserable in fact. Sarah knew exactly what the date was and woke in an expectant mood. She hurried to her office early and pretended to work on papers.

Her morning class ran into some difficulties with an assignment, and everyone seemed to be on edge. A third of her students were absent. Many lived near the coast so returned home to help their families prepare for the storm.

Several students disagreed on the meaning of some lyrics they heard in the previous class session. One student swore she turned in her assignment when Sarah told her she had a zero at that point. The girl argued—nicely—but argued, nonetheless. At the end of the class, the student approached Sarah and held out several pages.

"I'm sorry, Dr. Malloy. I thought I turned this in.

Honestly. But I found it just now, crumpled in the bottom of my backpack." Tears fluttered on the edge of the girl's lashes.

"Thank you, Cindy. I'm so glad you found it. That proves you not only did it but owned up to the mistake of saying you knew you turned it in. I will have to count off a few points for being late, but that's better than a zero."

Sarah developed a headache that even eating lunch didn't help. Several aspirins and some soothing music in her office helped more. The hall outside her office was quiet that afternoon. Even Danny and Bridget didn't show up.

A knock forced her out of a nap.

"May I come in?" Sergeant Tremont stood at the door.

"Certainly. You caught me napping. I've got a splitting headache."

"Best go home, Dr. Malloy, while you can. By nightfall, the rain will set in hard. That little car of yours may have trouble getting home."

"I hadn't thought of that. Good point. I'll leave as soon as I can." She meant she'd leave as soon as Reagan's photo showed up. "Can I help you with anything, or are you just making sure all the academics are safe?"

"Both as a matter of fact. Classes this afternoon have been cancelled in case you didn't get the memo."

"I hadn't. Haven't checked the computer since lunch."

"And I wanted to tell you what the final report was on that box you received."

Sarah sat up straighter and gestured to Bridget's chair that was closest.

"As we anticipated, the only prints were the ones we expected to find. The receptionist, yours, and your teaching assistant. Whoever left the box wore gloves which pretty much means most of the people around that day. The box was a standard gift box—cheap. The wrapping paper looked like it might have been used before but still no prints other than the ones I mentioned. The clay heart gave up nothing either. Standard kid's clay. Regular computer paper for the note." Tremont shook his head and apologized. "I'd like to have better news, but that's all we have. Has anything else odd shown up?"

"Nothing. To be honest, I think it's a prank or someone with a crush."

"You can't just blow this off, Dr. Malloy. You have to take precautions. As a matter of fact, where's that young woman who was here before? She seemed pretty emphatic about protecting you."

"Bridget? She's in her dorm. This weather brought on a migraine. She's lying with sound cancelling headphones and a shade over her eyes. Her migraines are that bad. My other teacher assistant, Danny, drove home last night. His parents live right on the beach. His dad is disabled. Danny's helping them relocate to his sister's house in Pennsylvania until this weather blows over, and they know the house is safe. Most of my students were absent this morning. Maybe they got the memo about afternoon classes before I did." She gave him a wan smile. "I think I'll go home soon. My headache is probably weather-related as well. I have no desire to ride out a hurricane in an academic building."

"I hear you. But I'll be here to guard the place. No looting if I can help it." He stood and moved to the door. "Be safe, Dr. Malloy." He touched the bill of his cap and left.

She rubbed her forehead with her eyes closed. Maybe a migraine headache was coming on with her as well.

The sound of someone clearing his voice startled her. A man in a uniform stood at her office door. Glancing at the clock, she could see it was about four in the afternoon. Seeing the package he held out to her, she signed quickly then returned to her chair. The sky had darkened, leaving her office in shadows. Sarah reached over and snapped on the lamp on her desk. She smiled at how the soft illumination fell on Reagan's picture. Kissing her fingertips then placing the kiss on his printed mouth, she started unwrapping the brown paper.

She should be used to surprises by now, but Sarah found that once more Reagan managed to delight her. This was an elegant picture. She sat on the couch, the lamp on the other side of her spilling soft yellow light across the side of her face, neck and gown. However, the focus of the photograph was the glass filled with amber liquid that she held in her hand. Sarah and the lamp were unfocused whereas the wine glass was front and center, in sharp focus. The lamplight shone through the wine and splintered into a thousand multi-colored diamonds. It was incredible how Reagan's camera captured that image. Where the colors were gold, orange and tan everywhere in the picture, a thousand different shades glowed from that crystal goblet. The picture was deep, textured, and rich, showing an eye for visuals such as Sarah had never seen. Oh, she knew she was in the picture, but the woman there wasn't what drew and held the eye...it was that glass caught at the most perfect moment. She admired the print for quite a while before turning it over.

September 2015

My darling Sarah,

I'm ducking bullets in Kenya these days. Thought I'd better be the one to tell you before someone else did. I'm all right, working on a poaching shoot. I'm very pleased with this shot. You make quite an elegant subject, but the glass of wine is the real focus. You know that. Your letters are incredible, especially the one where you shared your dreams...your very erotic dreams, I might add. Sarah, you have no idea what I did after I read what you were thinking that afternoon as you looked at my picture. I wanted to bury myself in your body so badly, love. But you weren't here. I remembered what you felt like...I remembered.

Love, Reagan

Sarah reached up and wiped the tears off her cheeks. She hadn't even realized she was crying until a drop of the salty substance rolled across her lips. Laying a hand on her chest, she pressed that spot where her heart was because she knew it hurt to read his words. Every time he wrote, he said more and more about how he felt. But he never asked for a commitment from her, nor did he give one. Sarah left her office early that evening. The weather was as bad as Sergeant Tremont predicted.

She drove into her garage, closed and locked the big door then took Reagan's latest photo into the house. Comfortable clothes. Tasty snacks. Safe as she could be from the storm, she poured a glass of red wine then held it to the light.

Memories flooded her. "Oh Reagan, if only you were here right now, snapping photos with that camera of yours. We'd finish the wine then let our love burst into a million colors just as the light through this wine does."

———

The next day Dr. Malloy noticed her students called greetings to her as they passed her door. Often the kids stuck their heads in the door and spoke for a minute or two before moving on. One young lady who was struggling with Sarah's latest assignment stepped into the office but came to a halt when she spotted the newest print on the doctor's desk.

"Is that the latest photograph from Mr. Conley, Dr. Malloy?" she asked. When Sarah nodded, the girl continued to stand there. Sarah waited to see what would happen next. "You love him, don't you, Dr. Malloy?" was the unexpected question. The teacher and the student looked each other square in the eye. No use denying it, Sarah thought; she did love Reagan Conley.

"Yes, Laura, I do love Reagan Conley." That's all Sarah intended to say on the subject. Let the kid fill in the details for herself.

"He loves you too, Dr. M." Laura turned her head so she could take in the prints Reagan had sent to Sarah since her return from Australia.

Now the girl had Sarah's complete attention. "What makes you think Mr. Conley loves me, Laura?"

"It took a while to figure it out, but I finally did. I've looked at all the prints you have of his work hanging in the classroom and here on the walls of your office. There is incredible skills and artistry reflected in every one of them. That's what makes his work so well known, so famous. But when you look at the photographs on your desk, well, the ones *he* took anyway, there's more than just skill. He put his heart into those shots. He poured his soul into making them perfect...for you. I don't know if he's a big talker or not. He might not be able to say what he feels, but he shows it, every time he sends one of these to you. It's kind of like, well, he's sending you his soul or his heart, one picture at a time." Laura blushed a little and looked uncomfortable. But she didn't stammer nor retract anything she said. It came from the heart.

Sarah looked at the young woman then looked at the framed images on her desk. She believed what the girl said. Reagan used his heart to see these pictures. Sarah very much wanted to believe that this man loved her enough to send these small tokens of his heart.

"Thank you, Laura," Sarah said in a quiet soft whisper, "You have no idea how much your words mean to me. These pictures speak to *my* heart...and now I know why. You're a very wise woman."

Laura ducked her head in acknowledgement of the compliment, backed out of the office and pulled the door closed as she left. Sarah sat looking at each print, touching here and there just to visit a spot that particularly appealed to her.

"I do love you, Reagan. If only you would come home."

Home. The meaning of *home* changed at that moment in Sarah's heart forever. *Home* was where Reagan was, whether it was in a jungle, desert or the skyscrapers of a metropolitan city. She sat thinking until the CD that played softly in the background caught her attention. The Beatles CD...she listened...*The Long and Winding Road*. Sighing, Sarah sang along with the song as she recalled the conversation she had with Reagan on the beach that first day together. Sometimes for someone you love, the *destination* is what the trip is all about, especially if you know what's waiting for you at the end of that journey. All Sarah wanted to do now was find Reagan and tell him she loved him. Everything else would take care of itself after that.

She wasn't going to say it in a letter. Sarah wanted to be face-to-face with him so he would know she meant every word she said.

———

"I heard a new picture came in."

Tom Penning managed to startle all three people in the office. Bridget gasped, and Danny dropped a pile of papers, causing a rather rude comment.

"Damn, don't you know how to knock?"

Penning ignored the two students and stomped over to Sarah's desk.

Rather than let him loom over her while she sat, she pushed her chair back and stood. "What comes into this office really isn't any of your business, Mr. Penning, unless it has your name on it," she pointed out.

He reached into his backpack, pulled out several rumpled pages and thrust them at her. "Read this and see if the characters are better."

She didn't take the pages but held up a hand to stop both Bridget and Danny from rising and coming to her side.

"You may leave them here and return in an hour. That will give me time to finish these essays and review your work." She gave him no other option.

"But I need that information now!" He stepped closer, his teeth bared.

"Then you should have come to my office sooner. An hour, Mr. Penning. That's all I have today."

"I bet you'd give him more than an hour." Penning pointed his middle finger at Reagan's photo but left almost on the run.

"He's dangerous, Doc." Danny moved to her side, both of them watching the door.

"I don't think he's dangerous, but he's certainly impulsive and irresponsible."

"I don't like him coming here. He gives me the creeps." Bridget shivered, a gesture that had nothing to do with the temperature outside.

"I'm not going to tell him he can't return. I'll simply have to control his visits more carefully."

"I'd feel better if you ignored him, Doc." Danny closed the door, his hand on the lock.

"Don't lock it. Others come in who legitimately need

help. Just forget him. He's a hothead and not a very nice person, but we can handle that."

Danny returned to his chair and began gathering the papers he dropped. "I hope you're right, Doc. Otherwise, we have a nutter on our hands."

———

Fall leaves slipped off the beautiful oaks on campus, and everyone wore jackets to ward off the cold. Despite the temperature, the sun shone most days so brightly that it hurt a person's eyes. Sarah loved autumn the most. There was something clean and crisp in the air that made her feel alive. She wrote letters to Reagan describing the changing season. Told him about covering her little MG in the heated garage and driving the bigger SUV for safety and warmth. She shared bits of students' essays. Funny stories about her colleagues. How she ate hearty soups and drank a small glass of wine each night, in remembrance of the time they spent together.

Words of encouragement, cheer and love laced each letter. Her confidence in her love for this man grew every day. She *would* see him again one day. Sarah lived for that day.

No matter what she wrote in her letters, however, she never mentioned Tom Penning. The young man worried her. Didn't scare her like he did Bridget. The man had a problem. Creativity wasn't one of them. He wrote well, if inconsistent at times. Reagan had real life and death things to worry about in his work. Sarah did not intend adding this piddling matter to that.

———

When October fifteenth rolled around, Sarah, Danny and Bridget were busy grading mid-semester exams. Papers lay all over the office, and anyone disturbing a stack did so at the risk of his or her own life. They grumbled at each other; each one aggravated with the other. It was tight working conditions, and they had a deadline to meet that Sarah had set for returning the graded exams to her students.

"I don't know about you two, but I've earned my salary for the day," Danny said as he laid another essay aside.

"We're behind schedule. How about I order pizza and pop."

"Is it that late? God yes, I'm starving!" Danny startled, realizing the day was slipping away, and his time ended at five.

When a deliveryman knocked on the office door, all three turned to answer it, expecting the food. Only this package wasn't food. At least it wasn't food for the stomach, just soul food for Sarah's heart.

"I forgot what day it was. Reagan's print arrived, right on time. Damn, that man is predictable. God bless the mail service wherever that package came from." Sarah rushed to the door, signed and gave Danny and Bridget a wicked wink. Grinning mischievously, she took her arm and made a wide sweep across the top of her desk. Papers didn't exactly flutter to the floor, but they did pile up close to the edge of the desk. Sarah could have cared less. She just wanted space enough to lay down the print.

In the midst of all the paper shuffling, the pizza man arrived. Bridget practically jerked the food from his hand while filling his other hand with dollar bills. Ungraciously she slammed the door in the poor man's face.

"That was rude, and I'll apologize next time I see him, but..." Bridget stood there with a large hot pizza in one hand and a bag with drinks in it in the other. She used her foot to drag her chair to the left of Sarah's desk. Danny already sat on the right side. And then they sat there in a quandary.

"Which first? The food or Reagan's photograph?" Sarah

knew what she wanted to do, but she waited to let the students make the choice. Looking at each other, Bridget laid the food to one side and scooted closer to Sarah's side while Danny moved his chair closer to the other side.

Like partners in crime, they huddled over that package as Sarah unwrapped it. Glancing at the mailing stamp, Sarah commented, "I'm not familiar with that particular stamp, but then they've all looked unfamiliar. It's like Where in the World is Reagan Conley?" They laughed over her small joke, but Danny bumped her arm.

"Get a move on, Doc. The suspense is killing me."

Despite all the haste to unwrap the print, Sarah slowed down just as she prepared to move the top piece of cardboard. She *never* knew what to expect, but she was *never* disappointed. Almost reverently, she unveiled the latest Conley masterpiece.

This time, no one spoke. Not a word. Sarah blushed. So did Danny, but Bridget only squirmed in her chair then sighed.

"Oops." Sarah offered as a way to ease their discomfort. "Reagan didn't take this photograph. I did," she explained.

It was the essence of manhood to her way of thinking. Sarah remembered taking two pictures of Reagan that he knew nothing about. One she already had on her desk, the study of shadow and light in his bedroom while he slept. She had taken this one earlier that same evening.

She woke up after she and Reagan made love late Sunday evening. He wasn't in bed with her, and she turned to locate him. The double doors of the bedroom were open, and she could see the setting sun on the horizon. It was a particularly spectacular sunset that night. Lavender, pink, blue and gold filled the sky. It was easy to find Reagan. He stood between her and the sun where it lay just on the horizon, that sun which was perhaps a few minutes from setting.

Reagan stood naked at the terrace rail. He must have gotten up and gone out to admire the view. From the bed where Sarah lay, it was like looking at a perfect picture already framed by billowing white curtains that fluttered at the sides of the doors. She reached over for the camera lying near the bed and turned it on. Focusing on Reagan, she adjusted the lens and waited. For what she wasn't sure; she just waited. And Sarah was glad she did. It was odd how coincidence worked.

Where Reagan stood at the rail, one couldn't tell he wore nothing. He stood silhouetted against the colors of the dying sun. The rail ran across the scene at his hips. Just as the fading light was its most colorful, Reagan took a broad stance, raised both arms out beside his head and stretched his entire beautiful masculine body. Sarah snapped the picture.

Seeing the shot now, she understood what he meant when he said one had to be prepared for that spur of the moment picture. Laying the camera back in its place, Sarah waited in bed for her lover to return. It was a bittersweet time for each of them. He was leaving. She was staying. They comforted each other that night.

Sarah sat in a trance, reliving that moment when she took Reagan's picture. Knowing she could tell these two things she wouldn't ordinarily tell others, Sarah nonchalantly told them what Reagan said about always having a camera ready for any picture that came up unexpectedly. She laughed a little and shrugged her shoulders.

"This was one of those moments I couldn't let pass."

She wiggled her brows up and down in a wickedly sensual way. "I wonder what Reagan thought when he saw *this* one?"

That struck Bridget and Danny as funny. They started laughing and drew Sarah into the merriment as well. Though they didn't say any more about how Mr. Conley might feel about having a picture made of his backside, the two young people would look at this print once in a while and chuckle.

She turned the photo this way and that. "No getting around it. This shot might be a bit too risqué for the office. It goes home with me tonight." Before they began eating, Sarah cut off the stamp and added it to the others in her desk drawer. After she propped up the print out of the way, Sarah brought out the pizza and drinks. They ate then called it a night.

Since she had the SUV, she dropped Danny then Bridget off at their dorms. The sun had gone down an hour before, and a cloudy sky covered the moon. She drove home in a good mood, anxious to get inside, get comfortable and warm so she could read Reagan's letter.

Wasn't it funny how she could put that off until she was alone and ready? Sarah never had to rush to read that short message; she knew it was there. She could wait. The stamp she'd put in her drawer looked Spanish. Maybe Reagan was in Europe somewhere. Hopefully he wasn't in Russia still.

October 2015

My darling Sarah,

I can't believe that picture! I almost didn't send it, but I knew you would want to see it, even if you see a little more of me than might be good for that desk in your office...your punishment for taking a picture of a naked man. I'm writing this letter on a plane. The pilot snatched me out from a South American country coup! He promised he'd mail this for me 'cause I have to return for some photos. I promise to take care of myself. I have too much of my life ahead of me and I don't want to miss a minute of it. I think of the Beatles' song, Long and Winding Road. The journey is interesting but I'm not sure what that destination is.

Maybe I'll find out soon. Enjoy my naked butt, you wicked woman!
   Love, Reagan

Reagan has been doing some heavy thinking, it seems.

Sarah wondered what conclusions he came up with. Then it dawned on her that he mentioned being snatched from the middle of a coup...that meant shooting, killing, civil dispute. Was he safe? Damn that man! He might not court danger, but it seemed danger didn't mind seeking him out. Sarah went to bed that night—not to sleep—with a sick feeling in her stomach. She could only pray he would be okay.

Chapter Twelve

"Sorry, not working with anyone today. Head cold that has my brain in a fog," Sarah called to whoever stood at her office door. She never even raised her head from the assignment she was creating.

"You'll see me." Tom Penning strode in as if he owned the place.

"That's high handed of you, Mr. Penning." Sarah didn't feel good. Danny and Bridget had a major test scheduled at the same time. Thus, her reasoning for having no one in the office with her. "I might even add that your lack of empathy for my health does not endear you to me."

"I have no empathy, Sarah. Haven't you noticed?"

"Dr. Malloy to you, sir. I will not accept anything less from students." By now, Sarah stood toe-to-toe with Penning, her gaze hard and her tone confident.

"You seem to expect me to be at your beck and call yet you ignore social distances like the fact I did not invite you in." His behavior bordered on total disrespect.

"I'm almost finished with my novel, and you need to check the last three pages before I send them in." He took

Danny's chair once again and started digging through his pack.

"I have no time today for reading your work."

"I think you do." Penning never raised his head until he pulled several pages out. He stood, walked to her desk and laid them down with a decided thump.

"Not today. I'll read them later and give you my opinion tomorrow morning before first class. You can meet me there." That would limit her time with him. "Once this novel is complete and you send it off, we'll have no more business to conduct. I'll ask you not to return to my office."

Penning took a step back and sent his gaze down her body then back up. Then he focused on the photos gathered on her desk. "It's because of him, isn't it? That you don't want me in here."

"What? No, that has nothing to do with Reagan Conley. This has to do with being rude, impulsive and aggressive. I pick whom I associate with, and I choose those who are positive. You, Mr. Penning, are not. You disturb the very air in here." By now, Sarah was in no mood to put up with him or his behavior. Though she was alone, the door was open. Several other faculty members were within ear shout. Penning didn't scare her. He disgusted her.

"I can't imagine how I allowed myself to be caught up with you, Mr. Penning. I will honor my word. I'll read this and give you my thoughts tomorrow morning. I wish you well on this literary journey you're on, but this office and myself are not your final destination." When in doubt pull out the Beatles, she decided.

"I'm not happy with you, Sarah. I'll see you tomorrow morning." Penning pointed his finger at her as he swung his backpack up to his shoulder, barely missing hitting Sarah.

To speak now would only add to his anger, so Sarah remained quiet. He marched out of her office but left a distinctly bad vibe behind. Sarah debated closing and locking the door or leaving it open. Finally, she decided she'd leave the door open. She only had forty-five more minutes in the office anyway.

Once more seated at her desk, she ignored the pages Penning left on the corner. She turned to her laptop and Goggled personal security devices.

Not far from the university was a tech store, filled with possibilities for her safety. She honestly didn't think Penning would bother her after she handed over those last pages and gave him her opinion. However, there was no sense in denying the man seemed a bit unhinged at times. Maybe he was bipolar. One day on meds, he was as right as rain. One day without meds, he was like a different person. It happened.

A trip to this tech store was on her agenda as soon as she locked up and cleared campus. Before she could gather her stuff—including those pages that she had yet to pick up, a knock came at her door.

"Sarah, do you have a moment?" Dr. Jean Cramer, who had an office down the hall, stood there.

"Certainly, Jean. How can I help? Come in. Take a seat." Sarah pulled Bridget's chair to her desk, and the women sat, facing each other.

"What are these?" Jean spotted the papers Penning left on Sarah's desk. "Is this from Tom Penning?"

"Yes, he's almost finished with a novel that a publisher wants. He has a deadline, and I've read a few pages to help him keep his characters on the plot's straight and narrow. I had him in a class last winter. He's apparently stuck with it since he's here and working on this." She laid a hand on the pages.

"Sarah, I'm not sure you understand Penning. He's not taking classes here this semester. He works as a stocker for a warehouse locally. As for writing a novel or having a publisher, he's lying."

"What? How do you know this, Jean?"

"He did the same thing to me this past summer. He wasn't enrolled but acted like he was. He wanted me to check out some work a publisher wanted. He had a deadline to meet so pressured me a lot until I put a halt to it. Frankly, the man scared me to death toward the end. I did some checking. He attends no classes. He has no novel, and there is no publisher."

"And how did you check on all this?" The information Jean shared amazed Sarah.

"I hired a friend who is a private investigator to follow Penning and find out what his life is like at that time. He's low key, has few if any friends, goes nowhere, and speaks to no one. Which is why my friend thought Penning coming to me all the time was odd. I put a stop to our meeting at the PI's insistence."

"I've already told Penning that I'll return these pages with my opinion tomorrow morning outside my classroom but that he's not to come here anymore and that we have nothing more to do with each other."

"I must say you're a braver woman than me. And a smarter one too. I remained on his hook, dangling like a stupid guppy, for almost two months." Jean stood. "I had an academic question to discuss with you, but I think I'll wait until tomorrow. Take care, Sarah. Be careful." Jean left as quickly as she came, but she left Sarah more convinced that a personal security device might be a very good idea.

———

Sarah laid a small box on Bridget's desk the next morning. She'd come to school extra early in order to get ready for her class but more importantly to prepare for her meeting with Tom Penning. She didn't expect trouble in the middle of the hallway, but then disappointed people often act out without thinking of consequences first. Penning probably fell into that category—act first, think second.

She'd bought two things at the tech store the night before. Thankfully the men who worked there were ex-military and experts in security. Her request struck them as odd, her trying to protect herself by her own means rather than put the police on alert in case this person became irrational or violent. She assured them that she'd dealt with unruly students before, and this student seemed little different from those.

So this morning in that soft light that shadows trees and buildings before the sun rises, she gathered papers, her purse and calendar. She carried that so students could schedule office meeting with her without coming by.

The last thing she did was place that box on Bridget's desk. Inside was a tracking monitor that would follow the device she had tucked into her bra. The second thing Sarah bought was a burner phone she got at the last minute. She'd carry that and leave her personal cell in the box, the tracking app set to locate the burner. The burner and tracking device weren't large so she tucked the small burner into the tall boots she chose to wear this day.

Not only was the weather miserable, cold and blustery, but a major storm was moving in. The university had already sent out a notice to staff and students that classes would be canceled the next day and possibly the day after.

Bridget and Danny would be in the office all day, grading, filing and doing what they generally did. One of them would find the package labeled:

Open this if you can't get hold of me. Burner number: 609-945-128. DO a TRACE. Do NOT call directly. Call the police if I am missing.

* * *

Maybe this is overkill. Maybe I'm letting my writer's imagination carry me away into a fantasy land.

Maybe she was paranoid but better prepared than not. For the first time since her meeting with Reagan, she did not think of him. Now it was on her to keep this journey going. If danger found him occasionally, danger would not find her ill-prepared if it came calling.

Closing her office door and locking it, she made her way down the central staircase, headed across campus to her classroom. The sky wasn't quite light yet. Shadows still lurked in corners. The brittle cold air bit into her skin. Somewhere behind her, a noise caught her attention, something that shouldn't have been there.

She turned, but a hand came around her face, covering her nose and mouth.

"Hel..." Her words faded, and she slumped unconscious.

———

Waking took effort. Whatever knocked her out lasted a long time. Her mind moved slowly. Her mouth was dry. Her eyes moved side to side, but her eyelids wouldn't open properly. She lay on a soft pallet or bed. The air around her touched her face with icy fingers. No heat. Total quiet. No traffic sounds. Finally, her eyelids opened enough so she could see through slits.

What she saw made no sense. Wooden walls. One window opposite her, the panes covered with some sort of cloth. The entire place as far as she could make out from lying flat on her back was no more than ten by ten. At least the panes appeared intact. She saw no cracks in the glass. The roof too was intact. But the walls must have been only that. A single layer of wood to stop the incessant cold. Cold that would get worse in the coming hours if she didn't get away.

If you watch enough TV and/or read enough mystery murder books, you quickly realize that you're in deep shit. Trouble with a capital T. Someone knocked her unconscious then brought her here. Her best guess would be somewhere deep in a forest. Maybe in a hunting cabin.

But where?

And who?

Sarah turned her head enough to see the rest of the place. A wood burning stove stood across the room, a kettle sitting on its top plate. From the feel of the room, no one had yet started a fire in the stove.

Time?

Late in the afternoon? A faint glow came through the single window at a low slant.

Across the room stood a sink of some kind, but Sarah could see no plumbing. Rough living here. And cold...deadly cold if no one came to start a fire.

She thought about sitting up. Getting her feet under her. Leaving this place.

That thought died when she discovered thick rope tied her hands and feet, her feet also tied to the ends of the iron bed on which she lay. If she made a great effort, maybe she could at least sit up. Struggling a bit, she turned onto one hip, then used her elbow to lift her body. She had to stop for a minute until her head stopped going round and round. Side effects, she figured, from whatever knocked her out. Eventually she managed to sit upright. But that was awkward with her feet tied in place.

"What the hell is going on here?" She spoke aloud thought no one but she occupied the cabin. "Where the hell am I?"

"Outside Toronto...about an eight-hour drive. No picnic driving in the dark with snow blowing," came a familiar voice from the door behind Sarah. Familiar, yet she had trouble connecting a name to the tone. The slight arrogance. The smugness.

A shadow passed her, then a man came in sight. He stopped at the end of the bed where Sarah sat. Like a stone statute, she sat with mouth open and eyes that widened.

"Unbelievable! You! What are you playing at? Cut me loose, and get me back to New Jersey!" Fury rose up in her and spewed out of her mouth. "What does this solve, you kidnapping me?"

"Oh, I don't know. I kind of like having you helpless," Tom Penning said as he leaned casually against the wooden wall and propped the toe of one boot against the floor.

"Helpless?" Sarah did some fast thinking. The opposite of *helpless* would be *self-reliant*. A person in control of his or her life, the world around him. No one was in control all the time. Yet this man seemed to think Sarah had control?

"Take me home immediately!"

"I don't think so."

"The police will be looking for me when I don't show up for class." That threat might work.

"Have you ever noticed that there are no cameras on the faculty parking lots? And if you park under a tree then it's even darker after the sun goes down. The only streetlight is at the other end of the section where you parked yesterday morning. Closer to your office but farther from any light." He moved away from the wall and sauntered around the tiny cabin, flicking his fingers over the table and two chairs, touching the stove.

"You watched me? Stalked me? Is that what this is about?" She had trouble understanding him. None of this made sense to her, but apparently, it made sense to Penning.

"Watched? Damn right! Stalking? Nah, *stalking* implies you're pestering someone or irritating them. I don't do that."

"Are you kidding me! That's exactly what you've been doing for the past few weeks."

"No, it isn't."

Sarah almost argued with him. Trying to make him see that his behavior was wrong wouldn't change him or the situation though. She should have listened to Bridget and Danny. The man had a problem. Some sort of disorder.

Time to change tactics.

"It's cold in here. The least you can do is start a fire in that stove, so I don't freeze to death while we wait for the police." Best to remind him of that.

He shrugged but didn't seem concerned.

"Aren't you worried they might hurt you when they arrest you? You're a kidnapper now. Besides that, you took me into another country though how you managed that I have no idea."

"I'm from around here. You get to know the countryside well when you do home schooling. If you're smart, then lessons don't take long so I would go exploring."

Familiar territory—the first thing police would check. Hope burned a slight bit brighter.

"This is wrong. You know that, don't you? You don't seem concerned about my health. I could freeze to death. You don't seem concerned about your health either. The police might not be kind when they show up." She talked reasonably to him but got a less than reasonable response.

"Shut up!" Penning slammed his fist against the door, rattling metal hinges. "Just shut up! I don't give a fuck about health. You can't do anything right now. Not so high and mighty huh. I didn't kidnap you. You drove off. Took your book bag, purse and phone in your car. No one's looking for you!" He stomped around the cabin, shouting at her.

Despite her assurance that someone would find her soon,

his attitude and irrational thinking scared her. She pulled back when he came close.

"Ah hah! That got you! You're frightened, aren't you!" He gloated, his face split with a wide grin, a pep in his step. His whole demeanor changed. "Not so smug now, are you?" He practically wallowed in his triumph.

"So..." Sarah hesitated to approach him again about the police. That might set him off, and she was tied up. He could do anything to her in this situation. "What kind of plan do you have, now that we're here?"

He stopped as if hitting a brick wall. "Plan?" The word held no meaning for him. "Plan? I have..." His steps took him to the door. Cutting a dazed glance back at her, he pulled the door open and shut it quietly which startled Sarah. She truly expected him to slam it.

Alone, Sarah slumped, something she'd never do in Penning's presence. She hoped the tracker was still tucked in her bra and that he hadn't discovered the burner phone tucked inside her boot. With hands tied, she had no way to check though.

"He kidnapped me, stole my car and took all my things." She had to give him some credit. He'd studied the parking lot and managed to get her away in her own vehicle, which might not arouse suspicion for a long time. Of course, she'd not be in class, and Danny or Bridget might realize quickly that something was wrong. For sure, one of them would when they went to the office and found that box.

While Reagan Conley hadn't entered her thoughts for hours, now she prayed that he never find out about this. Though the situation fell squarely on Tom Penning's shoulders, Reagan would be frantic about her. No telling what he might do to Penning when they caught up to him. Reagan had his own situations to worry about. If she escaped—she changed that to *when* she escaped, she'd have to control the media so he'd never find out.

Control...oops. There was that word.

Penning thinks I have total control, she mused. I wish. If I did, I'd be wherever in the world Reagan is, certainly not here. Not even at Princeton as much as I love it. If he traveled, I'd travel too.

Thinking of him helped keep fear tamped down.

I know Reagan is scared sometimes. He's all but admitted it in his messages. If he can face the fire and power through, then so can I.

Her resolve settled in her mind but did little to alleviate the real fear that she might freeze to death before being rescued. Or that that tech she bought wouldn't work like she was told it would. Or that Penning might kill her outright.

The shadows at the window faded into darkness. Sarah's coat sheltered her but wasn't heavy enough to keep her warm through the night. The weather was supposed to get worse. Or had that already happened? The darkness within the cabin was total now. Not even moonlight broke the gloom.

She heard the door open though she had no idea if the person coming through was Penning, a stranger or the police.

"Miss me?"

Penning. Damn! Her teeth chattered so hard that she couldn't have answered him if she wanted to. Not only that but she had to pee.

Something fell to the floor, startling her enough that she jumped. Something else small scratched, and suddenly the darkness gave way to a tiny light—a candle that Penning sat on the end of the table. What she heard earlier was the sound of logs dropped on the floor. He'd gathered wood.

She prayed he would start a fire. She had personal needs that needed attention as well.

"Mr. Penning, I have to go to the bathroom. Please."

He ignored her as he squatted in front of the stove, feeding in small pieces of thin twigs. He concentrated on building a fire, feeding larger pieces of wood into the belly of the iron stove.

Sarah didn't know whether to be grateful or ask for the bathroom again. The heat crept across the room, riding along the ceiling. She sat up the better to soak it up, but that crunched up her bladder.

"Mr. Penning, I have to pee." No sense being delicate. He didn't care. "Surely there's a spot in here where I can have a few minutes of privacy."

He ignored her.

"Tom Penning! I have to pee! Now!"

Penning jumped like someone kicked him. He whirled around and ran to the bed. He stood over her, his face mean, his lips pulled back and his eyes wild.

Without a word, he drew back a hand, pulled it around and slapped her across the side of the face so hard she flew back against the thin mattress, her ankles where they were tied to the bed frame screaming in pain. Her hands, tied as they were, flew over her head. The worst part, besides the unexpected pain, was the loss of bladder control. She wet herself. Her nose wrinkled, and she squirmed.

He recognized the signs, pushed her over to face the wall and cackled when he saw the moisture on her clothes and mattress. "Don't need that privacy now, do you, Sarah. Pissed all over yourself." He left her on her side and walked away.

Not willing to look at him anymore, her face in pain, Sarah stayed that way, the puny warmth, destined to lose against the brittle cold, chilled the wet that seeped across her backside. Tears slid down her face, across the bridge of her nose. One tear settled in her ear. She refused to shake her head to move it on. With her personal need brutally alleviated, she had no further reason to speak to Penning. Praying that someone would find her soon and that Reagan would never find out about this, she closed her eyes and slipped into a bone-chilling sleep.

Will I awake? Or will this be the big goodbye that writers add to their novel when a character dies?

Chapter Thirteen

While she slept, Penning apparently got cold too because a large stack of wood lay beside the stove when she woke and turned enough to locate him. He sat at the table, his backpack open on the other chair, papers scattered over the surface.

"Awake huh. Bet you have to pee again." His grin told her he'd be happy to solve that problem in the same manner as he did before. Turning back to his papers, he ignored her.

Sarah wanted to ignore him and soak up some of the heat she felt. While the cold assaulted her viciously, she could feel the heat. Flopping over onto her back, she stared at the window across from the foot of the bed.

Is that snow? I thought the really bad weather was over for a while.

"Mr. Penning, is it snowing?"

"Cranking out a blizzard across the lower part of Canada and the northeast. It's that dip in the jet stream everyone expected." He answered her while he continued to write, though he never mentioned Princeton or the text alert the university sent out—which he would have gotten if he were enrolled this semester. A fact, she decided, might be best to not mention.

"We could die here, you know." She wondered if he was aware of how insidious dropping temperatures could be. "We could go into shock from cold and never realize we're dying." Maybe scaring him would force him to relocate, preferably to a warmer place. Even better, if he went with the police and she could return home and forget this nightmare.

While Penning's pencil scratched, Sarah admitted that even if Reagan never found out about her being kidnapped—and that was a huge *if*—she'd never forget this... She didn't have a word to describe being kidnapped and worrying about peeing, freezing to death—

Her stomach growled, interrupting her morbid but honest concerns. "Do you have anything to eat?"

"Eat?" This time Tom Penning did look up, an odd expression on his face. "I uh..." He sat still as a stone, his focus off in some faraway place. "I don't think we have anything to eat."

"Oh great, you never planned to kidnap me. You never planned to haul me off to Canada in my own vehicle. You never planned to start a fire to keep us alive. Oh, and you never planned to bring food to keep us alive." She gave him an up and down glance, assessing him. Her snort came as she said, "You're a sorry planner, you know that?" She turned, giving him her back.

He may get angry again and come after me, she realized after she said what she said. Sarah, there are times when you really need to keep your mouth shut, you know.

Behind her, she heard him digging in his pack. More paper? A candy bar? What?

"Wish I had some coffee." He dumped the bag back on the chair and returned to his writing.

"Working on that non-existent novel for that pretend

publisher who gave you that fake printing deadline?" She spoke with her back to him. No way would she face him because eye-to-eye contact might get her killed.

"I have no idea what you're talking about."

His words said one thing, but the tone he used sounded less assured. Less confident.

"Whatever." She tossed his favorite word at him and ignored him. Or pretended to. She knew exactly what he was doing and where he was in that room at all times.

While on her side, she felt the corner of the tracker tucked in her bra. Hoping to give it better transmission ability, she turned onto her back. If a storm was raging like he said, that tracker signal might not get through.

"Mr. Penning, before this storm gets worse or we freeze to death, whichever comes first, I really would like to go outside and relieve myself. And I don't mean pee either."

"Seriously? Man, you must live in the bathroom."

This time he considered her request because he glanced at the door then at the window. Snow fell, but so far, the wind wasn't a factor.

"I'll take you to the back corner of the cabin, and you can squat there, but I have to be able to see something of you at all times. Stick your butt away from me."

He moved to the foot of the bed and began untying the rope around her ankles.

Maybe I can run faster than he can, she thought.

"Oh, and Sarah in case you think you can outrun me, keep this in mind. You have no idea where you are. A storm is almost here. And I'll hurt you real bad if you do try to escape. Just to make it a little easier for you, I'm tying your ankles back together but with enough length between them so you can sort of walk."

Sure enough, he kept the rope around one ankle and tied the other but left about twelve or fourteen inches between.

Not enough rope to run. Maybe not enough to even walk but she could shuffle, and that was good enough. As hard as it was to admit, Penning finally spoke the truth; she knew she could not survive alone in the coming storm. He could, and then he'd find her since he knew the area. Assuming, of course, that he told her the truth about being from here. At this point, she had trouble knowing whether he spoke honestly or not. The deluded man might not even recognize a truth or lie himself.

He hauled her to her feet but did give her time to orient her feet and equilibrium after lying down so long. When she stood steady, he grasped her upper arm and walked her to the door. The minute he opened it whatever heat the stove managed to generate fled, sucked out by a breeze that she knew might become a howling wind soon enough.

"Let's get this over with," he said as he hauled her down the two steps and guided her around the corner of the cabin. He took her to the back corner and turned her so her back was at the corner, and he could see her front. "Now do your thing while I do mine."

Crap! Does that mean he's going to poop too?

Not wanting to see what he might do, she wrestled with the narrow belt she wore, managed to pull down the thick wool slacks and squatted. Closing her eyes, she did her business. When she heard water running, she opened them enough to see Penning not far away, his side to her. Seems he had to pee as well. She snapped her eyes closed, did an almost-impossible feat of sticking her hands under her and using snow to clean her bottom. Stretching muscles in the oddest ways, she'd probably be sore in a million places after that—if she lived through Penning and the weather.

"All done I see," he said while she still wrestled with her belt. "Get along. We need to get inside before we freeze to death."

Only by the grace of God did Sarah avoid rolling her eyes. *Now* he's worried about the falling temperatures.

"Why don't we get into that car I saw behind the cabin, crank up the motor and leave?"

"Not happening."

"How come?" They neared the front steps when he turned her toward him.

"Miss Smarty-pants, that car is older than you and me together. It's covered with limbs and leaves. Probably hasn't moved in thirty years."

Confused, Sarah looked around him for another car or hers. "So how did we get here?"

"Your car is in a deserted parking lot. I borrowed another car that was parked there. Stupid driver left the thing unlocked. We drove near here. I dumped that pile of crap, and I carried you here." He jerked her up the steps and through the door, but he did take her to the chair where he'd sat earlier, near the stove. He moved to the other side of the table, keeping an eye on her. "When you warm up, you go back over there." He jerked his thumb toward the bed.

She nodded, afraid to anger him this time since she had the opportunity to warm up.

They must have stayed that way for an hour though she had no way to tell time.

He finally moved her back to the bed and retied her feet to the foot of the iron bed.

"Have you sent a ransom demand yet?"

He ignored her, once more scribbling.

"How are they delivering the money?"

His pencil slammed down on the table, but he didn't look up.

"Oh my god, you didn't plan for that either." She did roll her eyes this time, not caring whether he saw or not. "Mr. Penning, for a fairly bright but fairly troubled young man, you're a piss-poor kidnapper. We're either going to freeze to death or die of starvation and dehydration." Like a lightning bolt, she realized they *could* drink. "Hey genius, why not fill those cups over there with snow and melt it on the stove enough for us to get a drink."

Penning said nothing about Sarah coming up with a plan to keep them hydrated. But he did get the two cups and head to the door.

"And don't get any of that snow that you pissed in," she ordered. Maybe she could gradually take back control of this situation and talk him into releasing her. That was a long shot but the only thing she could think of to save herself and this nutter. Danny's word slipped into her mind so easily. For a second, she wanted to sob but knew that would make Penning happy so she sucked up the sobs and used the sleeve of her coat to wipe the tears from her eyes.

Just in time too.

Wind blew the door in so hard it bounced off the front wall. Two cups in hand, Penning fought to close the door.

"You're letting the heat out. Now you have to start all over again," Sarah said, letting her voice sound tired.

Penning grunted rather than come back with a retort.

Maybe I'm getting to him.

First, he stooped down and added more wood to the fire. It burned low at this point. Then he sat the cups on top of the stove, pulled up a chair and watched them. When the snow melted enough to drink, he used the corner of his coat to move both cups to the table. A few more minutes and he drank his as if it were ambrosia. A heavy sigh escaped him. He sat back in the chair and closed his eyes.

When did he last sleep? Did he sleep while I did? Sarah had something new to think about. What if he falls asleep and I can untie myself and get out of the cabin without waking him... She gave a big sigh. That was a pipe dream. Penning was

155

right about her escaping—she'd never survive even if she made it past him. And he'd hurt her and enjoy every minute.

"Do you think I might have some of that?"

Feeling the handle to see if the cup was cool enough to carry without using his coat to hold it, he brought the cup over. "I can pour it in your mouth while you lay there, but that might be a bit messy." His smirk said he'd enjoy her discomfort.

"I'll sit up, thank you." Sitting up was harder this time than the first time she tried. This time she had to contend with sore muscles that had been slapped and bent in undignified ways.

He held the cup to her mouth but didn't rush her. She drank deeply then used her hands to take the cup from him. Quickly he stepped back while she finished the best tasting water she'd ever had.

"That was good. Thank you. Can we have more?" She said *we* instead of *I*, including him in this miserable situation that was quickly turning into a bad situation.

With a quick look at the window, judging she assumed, how bad the storm was now, he snatched up both cups, edged sideways out the door and returned in less than thirty seconds, again edging through the door. Losing warmth to an open door at this point was not only stupid but possibly deathly.

This time he sat the cups on the table and returned to his writing.

She was hungry, but at least she'd had a drink. Sarah could survive as long as Penning remained stable and that stove kept going. The pile of logs would dwindle fast at this rate.

So many questions. Where's the log pile? Can you get there easily? Did you send a ransom demand? He never answered that question. She'd bet he didn't. Never gave it a thought. Just snatched her in the early morning pre-dawn and drove off to parts unknown. Well, unknown to everyone but him, if he were to be believed. When this storm is over, can we go somewhere else and get a warm bath and warmer food? What do you want from me?

Finally, she gave up trying to figure out Penning and finding answers. She let her mind roam to Reagan. Where are you, love? I hope it's warm and safe. I hope you have a plate of delicious food. I hope you think of me with love.

She drifted off to sleep but dozed fitfully, afraid that sleeping might become permanent. Twice Penning got up and fed more wood to the stove. Once she tried waking him to check the fire.

"Mr. Penning! Tom! Wake up! Check the fire."

Waking up was hard enough for Sarah. Tom Penning took forever to respond to her calling him, and he was closer to the warmth. By now, Sarah couldn't feel her feet, and her hands where she managed to tuck them into the folds of her coat were losing feeling.

Aroused at last, he checked the fire, tossed on the last logs and stood, stretching his length.

"Can you get to more logs?"

He didn't answer for a few seconds, but this time he wasn't ignoring her. "I think so. They're stacked up just around the corner. Depends on how bad the storm is."

"We'll need more real soon," she encouraged.

"Yeah, yeah, I know." His voice sounded groggy. Like he had trouble waking.

"We need lots of wood." Sarah kept on nagging. He'd either do as she suggested or get angry.

Taking a few clumsy steps to the door, Penning pulled his coat close, reached down and grabbed a gunny sack that someone threw into the corner.

Time goes fast when you're having fun, they say. Time right now moved like a turtle in a snowstorm. Slowly.

Eventually the door eased open, and Penning returned,

carrying a load of logs bundled up in the sack. "I can carry more using this. Storm's about over. The wind's laid. The snow isn't falling as hard or fast as before."

His words offered the first hope Sarah had heard in the last few days. "Maybe we can leave when the weather clears, and we can walk out."

Penning shrugged but said nothing as he fed more logs into the stove.

Several hours passed. Now that the storm passed, silence fell outside.

With the stove going constantly, the cabin was at least above freezing. Compared to what blew in every time the man went outside, the place was a veritable hot spot.

So cozy in fact that Tom sat writing at the table once again, immersed in his pretend novel. At least she imagined that's what he was writing.

She watched him to judge his mood, and while doing so, she thought she saw something move on the floor behind him. Oh joy, she thought, I bet he brought in a damn mouse. It was probably hiding in the woodpile. She groaned and that caught his attention.

"What's up?"

About to answer him, taunt him with bringing in vermin she might have to contend with while tied up, fear grabbed her by the throat and left her speechless. All she could do was use her hands to point, her eyes wide, her mouth working but nothing coming out.

Penning recognized terror when he saw it, no matter what kind of personal problems he suffered. He turned but saw nothing because the snake was curled around the front leg of his chair.

"Snake! Move!" Sarah screamed.

Penning had no clue where the snake was. He looked this way and that. By delaying those few heartbeats, he allowed it time to move down near his foot so the first—and last—thing he did was step on the snake's back end. With blinding speed, the viper whipped around and sank fangs into his leg, drew back and hit again. And a third time.

Penning screamed, shaking his leg. The snake landed near the stove, curled up and hissed. Penning backed up next to Sarah's bed, limping.

With humans on one side of the cabin and a snake on the other, that bad situation had now turned into a terrifying horror show.

"Tom, can you kill it?"

"I don't have anything to use!" Terror filled his words.

"Is it poisonous?"

"Massasauga rattler. Deadly. Hunts by finding heat. Like mice." He pulled a chair next to him.

Sarah thought he planned to use it to ward off the snake if it came near, but she quickly saw that he needed it for support.

"Tom, tell me how you're feeling right now."

"Shaky. Sick to my stomach. Cold."

Cold? Odd. They'd been in freezing temperatures for almost two day, yet Sarah saw sweat on his face. His skin was pale, and his hands were shaking where he held on to the chair.

Not sure whether to watch Tom or the snake, she opted to watch the snake. Whatever happened to Tom Penning would happen. But she and that snake were trapped. As long as it stayed by the stove, she might be okay, since the stove would provide heat and cover up *her* body heat. With her hands and feet tied, she presented a ready target if that thing began moving around the cabin.

A thud nearby sent her focus to Tom then back to the snake. He'd sat down, heavily. His eyes seemed glazed.

"Tom, do you have any health issues that might react with

that snake's venom?" Sarah had to know if he might crash on her.

"High blood pressure." His words sounded slurred. He sat so still, not at all like the young man she'd been dealing with.

"Medicine?"

"Yeah. Lisinopril." He slumped in the chair, his hands shaking.

"Tom, keep talking." Sarah's gaze vibrated back and forth between the snake still curled by the stove and the man who seemed to be fading right before her eyes. "Tom? Tom Penning, talk to me!" she yelled, even as his eyes closed, his body slumped further before leaning sideways and falling to the floor.

Sarah screamed bloody murder then as quickly she snapped her mouth shut. Eyes back on the snake now, she prayed it stayed across the room. She prayed the sun would stay up until rescue came. She prayed she didn't die here alone, struck by a snake, in the middle of nowhere.

The sun refused to answer her prayer. Slowly shadows moved across that one window.

The fire's going to die down soon. Tom can't feed it. Is he alive? Unconscious? I won't be able to see the snake when the sun goes down.

Her eyes hurt from watching the reptile. She squinted, finally realizing the sun was almost gone. Still the snake remained where it had landed. Near the stove that must still be warm if no longer hot.

Darkness never seemed so complete. Like velvet wrapped around the body. Soft. Delicate. Getting tighter with each hour until you couldn't breathe. Until you sweat in a room that had to be below freezing. Until you listened desperately for any noise that might sound like the syncopated rhythm of a sliding body coming closer, seeking more heat.

Did I sleep? Where's the snake? Damn!

Sarah snapped fully awake from a sound sleep, urgently seeking that snake. The corners of the cabin still lay in shadows so she imagined the damn thing everywhere she couldn't see clearly. She scanned her bed first. Nothing. Then she checked Tom. He still lay where he'd fallen. His color was gone.

He's dead. That's all she could think of. No consoling words. Nothing. Hoping the snake might have gone closer to him rather than her when the stove grew cold, she saw nothing threatening. How she wanted to look under her, bed but that was impossible. Her movements were small and careful, so as not to invite an attack from out of nowhere.

Her sigh cut short when she spotted a mottled pile on top of the stove. Despite the nighttime temperature, the stove must still be warmer than the floor. The snake crawled up on top and now lay curled there. It seemed in no hurry to move or even raise its head. However, that wouldn't last long once the stove lost all its residual heat.

Tears seeped from Sarah's lids. Which would come first— rescue or death. At this point, she figured it was 50-50 odds. The longer the day went on with her lying here helpless the less the odds would be in her favor.

Bright light shone through the windowpane, and Sarah lay on the bed counting blessings and regrets in her life. Blessings outnumbered regrets by a long shot. But the regrets were the ones that hurt her most. She never visited Sharon and Harvey Bannerman enough. She'd never told Danny and Bridget how much she admired, valued and eventually loved them. Nor how much she'd miss them when they graduated, first Bridget then Danny. She never spent enough time with her neighbor Sophie. She never invited Jean Cramer over to her house for dinner and an evening of wine and conversation.

She never told Reagan Conley that she loved him. That her life would be blessed every day if she could only be with him for as long as the gods allowed. Her heart hurt thinking of him. How he looked when he laughed. How he charmed people. How he loved her so tenderly. How that camera in his hand was an extension of his soul, and she was okay with that. How he'd blessed her life with those photos long before she met him.

So many blessings. So few regrets.

She'd almost accepted the situation, her death by freezing. She refused to accept the idea she'd die from snakebite, of all things, in some forest outside Toronto, Canada. Her mind dulled, her focus still on the snake, but with nothing else to do but wait, she lay on a cold bed, ready for whatever came next.

Boom! The door flew open. The wood splintered, and bodies in camo with guns rushed in.

"Snake! On the stove top! Kill it!" she screamed even as the viper raised its head and his rattles began shaking.

Boom! A thunder-like sound. A different kind of noise.

Two loud noises—the best sounds in the world. They meant she could live.

A man bundled in a coat zipped up to his nose approached Sarah, while one of the others removed the snake that he'd shot. The man in the coat held a blanket.

"Dr. Sarah Malloy?" He spoke with an accent. French perhaps?

She almost couldn't hear his question; her ears still rang from the door being destroyed and the gunshot.

"Sarah Malloy?"

"Yes, yes." Wanting to be strong, her answer came out so weak that the man had to lean closer to hear.

"I'm Detective James Grover, Toronto police. Is that Thomas Penning?" He nodded toward Tom's body even as he helped her sit up. Another man had a knife out, already cutting through the ropes holding her feet.

"Yes. The snake bit him. He had high blood pressure. I think he's dead."

Detective Grover threw the blanket around Sarah and moved aside slightly so that another man could cut her hand loose.

Blood returning hurt her hands and feet. She groaned and grimaced but gave the four men a smile. "Thank god! Thank god!" she told them before breaking down in heavy sobs.

Chapter Fourteen

"Réveillez-vous enfin." A nurse stood next to Sarah's bed. Seeing the perplexed expression, the nurse changed to English. "Awake finally." She smoothed the hair off Sarah's forehead. "You slept so long, cher. Let's get you cleaned up a little and perhaps a few bites of something soft and hot. Several wait outside to talk to you."

For the next thirty minutes, the nurse moved slowly, helping Sarah as she wiped her body then slipped into a clean hospital gown.

"A brush?" The nurse held out a hand with a tiny grin.

"I look a mess, don't I?"

"Oui," nurse said with a pretend frown that turned into a large grin.

Laughing aloud for the first time in a very long time, Sarah took the brush and used it to untangle her short curls. A sigh of gratitude escaped her as she laid the brush on the bedside table. "Am I presentable now?"

"Oui, mademoiselle. And now something hot to sip and a few bites to eat." The nurse pulled a rolling table across Sarah's bed and proceeded to uncover a cup of steaming broth and a small plate with that looked like grilled salmon. At the side was a pudding with blueberries.

Fork in hand, Sarah's mouth watered. The smell alone sent her into heaven. As she ate slowly, the nurse poured a cup of coffee from an insulated pitcher on the table. Sarah was quite sure she'd never had anything that tasted so good in her entire life.

Clean, freshly dressed and fed, she leaned back. Nurse had raised the head of the bed so she could speak with visitors easier.

"First you must speak to the detective. He has waited while you slept."

The nurse turned, but Sarah reached out a hand and stopped the woman. "Am I all right? How long did I sleep?"

The nurse patted Sarah's hand. "Vous allez bien...You are well, mademoiselle. You did sleep though for a full twenty-hours while your body returned to its normal temperature. Doctor will visit with you after lunch. Now I will fetch the detective."

Satisfied that she'd suffered no ill effects other than the lack of sleep—and a morbid respect for snakes and storms—and odd students—she sat back to await someone. She knew a man talked to her in the cabin. That she remembered. But nothing after that.

A slender man of medium height and brown hair knocked on her door. She waved him in with a smile. He approached her bed and smiled when she smiled at him.

"I don't remember your name, but I remember your eyes. Rich brown. I'm Sarah Malloy. Thank you for rescuing me."

"And I am Detective James Grover with the Toronto Police. Doctor says you are well?"

"Yes, the nurse confirmed I suffered no ill effects other than loss of sleep and perhaps near-hypothermia." Sarah folded her hands together on top of the blanket. "Can you tell me what happened after you broke down the door? I do remember that...oh and the shot!"

"Oui. May I sit, Dr. Malloy?" He gestured to the metal chair next to her bed.

"Certainly, sir." She waved him to the chair and laid her head back, prepared to hear the end of the story.

"Your plan worked perfectly. We would have found you perhaps a day sooner but for the storm. Traveling was danger-ous. The burner cell honed in on the tracker device almost immediately. Your assistants gave us the name of the man they thought might have taken you. We used the time in office to find out about him. Thomas Penning grew up near Toronto. His childhood was anything but ideal. He tromped the woods extensively. If you hadn't had that tracker, we might not have found you in time. The cabin was far back in thick woods."

"What about Tom Penning?" Sarah knew the answer but wanted to hear it from someone official.

"As you said he was dead. An autopsy showed the snake venom was at full strength. Combined with his high blood pressure, he went into shock almost immediately. He died within thirty minutes of the snake bites, according to our medical personnel."

Her head down, Sarah wanted to say a prayer for the misguided man but found she had no words. His final actions put her life in danger and that she had trouble forgiving.

"Thomas Penning was a troubled young man, Dr. Malloy. He'd been diagnosed with an antisocial personality disorder when he was in his teens. He managed to get into university and did well for some time, but for reasons we do not know, he fell back into his disorder and that led to his confrontations with you and your assistants." He paused then asked, "Do you know why he took you? We could find no motive for him kidnapping you. He sent no ransom note."

"I think...I think he wanted control over something. I

think he saw me as a person who had what he did not. Control. He seemed delighted that he had me tied up and helpless." She shrugged. "That's the only thing that ever made sense to me."

"You may very well be correct, mademoiselle, but we shall never know for sure."

"What about my car? He left it at some deserted parking lot? What about my purse and the things I was carrying?"

"We found your car. He left all your papers and your purse hidden in the back. However, he disposed of the key. An auto dealership has sent a replacement. You'll get that when you're discharged."

"So the kidnapping thing is over? I can go home when the doctor says so?"

"Oui. Arrangements have been made to transport you home comfortably and safely."

"Oh. That's wonderful. Thank you so much. I'm not sure how long I have to stay here though."

"Doctor Martin informed me that you should be released tomorrow."

"This may sound silly, Detective, but I have no idea what day this is or what date." Sarah blushed a little and used one hand to touch her burning cheek, only to discover that the side of her face still hurt."

"That bruising isn't as bad as you think, though your face will still show it when you return to classes, I suspect." Detective Grover motioned toward the left side of her face. "And today is Saturday, November seventh. Penning kidnapped you on Monday. We found you Thursday morning. We carried you out then the ambulance brought you to hospital. You slept for hours."

"And you waited." Her soft grin showed him she was grateful. "Thank you—and your men—for finding me. I worried that damn snake might get me first."

"If we might, mademoiselle, before I let your other visitors in, please take me through the entire timeline so we can close the case." He pulled out a notebook and pen then looked at her, his pen poised, ready to take down every detail.

A long and painful hour later, Detective Grover gave Sarah's hand a gentle shake as he wished her well and left. Nurse came in to check on her and reminded her that doctor would visit later. In the meantime, two more were outside waiting anxiously to see her.

"Who are they?" Sarah had no idea who might be here in Toronto wanting to see her other than the police.

"Un jeune homme et une jeune femme."

She knew just enough French to recognize *jeune femme*—a young woman?

"A young man and young woman, mademoiselle. I'll show them in now. They have been..." The nurse paused, considered her words then finished with a chuckle. "une douleur aux fesses." She opened the door but turned back to Sarah with a translation. "A pain in the butt."

That's how Danny and Bridget found Sarah, laughing hysterically in bed in a Canadian hospital.

"Doc, you okay?" Danny looked scared to death as he watched her laughter gradually peter off.

"Oh my, you are such welcome sights for sore eyes." Sarah held out her arms and embraced both of them at one time, awkward as that was. "I didn't mean to scare you with the laughing, but the nurse said you were *une douleur aux fesses*. A pain in the butt." That set her off again. "You must have given them fits out there."

The two assistants looked indignant at first then hung their heads in embarrassment.

"They wouldn't let us at least come back here and see that you were alive, Doc," Danny protested.

"And you doubted the word of a detective and a doctor?"

Sarah's funny bone had been turned loose, and she cackled again.

They finally settled the merriment, and Danny pulled up the recliner for Bridget while he took the less comfortable metal chair.

"Tell me what happened from your end, then I'll tell you what happened to me." Sarah encouraged them to calm down and understand that she was safe.

"You didn't show for class," Bridget began. "So we ran down to the parking lot which was on the way to the office. Your car wasn't there. Danny figured you might have had another flat or there was traffic, so as we headed to the office, he called your cell. No answer. He was still trying when we got to the office. I was unlocking the door when I heard a cell ringing inside. We thought you might be in there hurt but with the door locked, that seemed improbable. So we rushed in. By then the phone had stopped ringing. You and your cell weren't anywhere in there, so he called again. This time the ringing came from a box on my desk. God, Doc, that scared the bejesus out of me when I saw that note and opened the box to find your cell inside, ringing away."

"Neither of us wanted to try that tracing app so we called campus security, and they called the police. We hounded them pretty much day and night." Danny did a little head nod and grin at Bridget. "Maybe *pain in the butt* described us for a while."

"So you hung with the police as they used the app?" Sarah turned sideways in bed so she could see them better.

"We stuck like glue. The detective in Princeton got pissed at us, but I told him I got you in trouble with Penning to begin with, and I was going to help get you out." Danny's fierce expression showed he meant business.

"Now wait a minute. It's not your fault that Penning was a nutter. That he did stupid stuff." Sarah protested but saw quickly that she'd have a hard time convincing Danny that him letting Penning into the office didn't snowball into disaster. "I certainly don't blame you."

"He blames himself, Doc," Bridget said as she jerked a thumb at Danny. "He'll get over it once we're back in the office, and life returns to normal." She bent forward and lowered her voice. "Reagan Conley normal." She wagged her brows. "Understand what I'm saying?"

Clearing her throat in order not to laugh at the young woman, Sarah held out a hand to Bridget who squeezed it then to Danny who took it with hesitation. "Danny, no matter that you introduced Penning to my office, you helped find and save me from him. So don't feel guilty. I'm indebted to you both for saving me."

"Aw, Doc. We just nagged the police. Probably slowed them down. But yeah, that idea of tracking the burner they found in your boot was pure genius." Danny squirmed in his chair. "We're good, Doc?"

"Better than good." She saw the faces before her relax. And that reminded her of one of those regrets she thought of while tied to that bed in the cabin. "Danny, Bridget, I've never said how much I enjoy your company. Your contributions to work or the value you've added to my life. I've never told you how much I've come to love you both." Seeing the shocked expressions on their faces, she finished, "But I'm saying it now. I love you."

Bridget jumped up and embraced Sarah so hard the woman grunted. Both cried. Suddenly Bridget kissed her check then said, "Give me a minute, Doc," before she bolted out the door.

Danny stood, and Sarah held out her arms. He came into her embrace and gave her a gentle hug then stepped back. "I better check on my partner. She's been upset since you got 'napped. Me too," he added unnecessarily before he sauntered in apparent nonchalance out of the room, his hands tucked into his pockets.

———

Doctor Martin visited later in the afternoon, putting Sarah at the end of his list of patients while making his rounds.

"You were sleeping so soundly, mademoiselle Malloy, that I thought I'd visit you last."

"I can go home tomorrow?"

"Yes, your core body temperature has returned to normal. You suffered no permanent damage from hypothermia though your fingers and toes might still tingle for some time yet. At this point, sleep is the best thing for you."

"I'll have to make arrangements to return to Princeton." Sarah turned a worried face to him.

"There are some people here who will take you home in your own car. The detective told you they found it?"

"Yes, he did. Who will drive me?"

A knock on the door interrupted the conversation. Bridget peeped in. Danny leaned around her shoulder.

"Une douleur aux fesses," Doctor Martin said with fake disgust.

Sarah recognized the frown as fake because he then laughed. "I think I've heard that expression a few times when applied to those two." She waved the two in but stretched out her hand to the doctor. "Thank you for everything, sir. Merci."

"De rien. You are welcome, mademoiselle. Bonne chance." He left, nodding to the younger couple.

She needed no translation to know the doctor wished her good luck. "He says I can go home tomorrow, but no one's told me yet how I'm getting there other than I'll be comfortable and safe." She held up both hands, palms up, a puzzled expression on her face.

Danny reached into his pocket and pulled out a single key fob. "Guess who's driving first?"

"You? You and Bridget are driving me home?"

At their identical nods, she sighed and laid back. "How perfect."

————

The assistants drove Sarah home in her own Subaru, taking care not to wear her out, though Sarah slept the biggest part of the eight-hour drive. Once home, Bridget pulled the SUV into the garage then helped Sarah into the house.

"What else can we do for you, Doc.?"

She rested in her recliner with a lap quilt across her legs. "I'm good, guys. Thanks. Now you get home, and take care of your own business." She sent them on their way with a kiss and hug apiece.

"Hey, Doc, use that delivery service to get something to eat. That way you don't have to go out," Danny told her as he closed the front door and headed to the Uber cab Bridget had called.

Taking his advice, she got a delivery of soup and sandwich with a big slice of cheesecake for dessert. Making hot tea, she returned to her recliner, ate then pulled paper, pen and a writing lapboard to her.

While the T. A.s drove her home, she did some thinking. As much as she didn't want Reagan to know what happened so he'd not worry about her, she didn't want a relationship based on lies. Omitting this crisis would be a lie. She would put it all in a letter to him.

November 2015

My dearest,

Life is full of surprises, and I've suffered a nasty one. It's over now, and I'm safe. The police, Danny and Bridget saved me. I'm going to tell you all in this letter though at one point when things looked hopeless, I prayed you'd never find out about this. Life on your long winding road is filled with danger that thankfully misses you. I didn't want to add to your worries. But then I realized our relationship, whatever this is, must be based on truth. Not telling you what happened would be a lie by omission. And I'll not have that. Ever.

So let me tell you about Thomas Penning...

Sarah wrote for an hour, taking time to word her story carefully so that Reagan would understand as she went along that it was over and she was alive and safe.

And there you have the entire story, darling. I am safe, thanks to the efforts of Danny and Bridget who jumped right into action, and the police who did a marvelous job of tracking down Penning and me. The only hiccup in the story was the damn weather. Otherwise, I would have been home within a day, rather than two. Other than having a healthy respect for and a fear of rattlesnakes, I'm fine. I miss you so much.

Love, Sarah

————

Sarah rolled over in bed several mornings later to see a dull gray sky and snow falling. No wind blew the powdery flakes;

they fell in a straight line. The house floors were cold beneath her feet. She grumbled but realized she'd been colder so gave up the complaint. Even her shower didn't warm her spirits. Sarah moved in a kind of *blue funk*.

Traffic hadn't picked up in her usually quiet neighborhood. Her sturdy SUV with its new tires and snow chains eased its way to the campus where she parked and walked up the sidewalk to her office. Even with students and faculty moving along the paths, the campus was so quiet that she could hear the snow hitting the tree leaves and settling on the ground. Today she wished she were anywhere else in the world but here. No, actually that wasn't quite right either. She knew where she'd like to be, back at the bungalow above the white-hot sands waiting for Reagan to join her out on the terrace.

She surprised herself by wiping a single tear off her cheek. Despite the beauty of the snowfall and the peaceful silence, Sarah was depressed. Turning her face up to the snow, she let the flakes land then melt on her skin. Shaking off the moisture on her cheeks, she walked in to the building to her corner office.

After her morning class, Sarah returned to the office with an armload of books, CDs and papers. Pushing the half-closed door further open, she entered to find Bridget sitting at her desk in her high-backed chair. The girl leaned forward with her chin resting on both fists and her elbows propped on the desktop.

Hearing Sarah enter, Bridget startled and made to get up.

"No, stay where you are, Bridget. I've got to file these papers and put things away. You're okay where you are for now." Noticing two of Reagan's photographs pulled to stand in front of Bridget there on the desk, Sarah pulled open a filing cabinet and began shuffling papers. "What's up, Bridget?"

The young woman sighed before she spoke. "Dr. M., you

wear those heart earrings all the time." Bridget looked over her shoulder as she spoke. Sarah nodded. Turning back to look at the framed prints, Bridget once more put her chin on her fists as if she pondered what she saw.

Something's on her mind.

Sarah worked and waited to hear what the matter was. Bridget just sat though. She finished her filing then turned to put the CDs in their cases. Bridget jumped as if she forgot the doctor was in the room.

"See that necklace?" Bridget finally said.

"Yes," Sarah drew out her answer.

"Well, it's in two of these pictures...the one where you're sitting on the bed reading the newspaper and the one with the wine glass. Now, I can see you wearing the thing if you're all dressed up because it's a stunning piece of jewelry. But if you're wearing it when you have practically nothing else on, then that means the necklace is special to you. Right?"

Sarah nodded again, but tears welled and spilled over her lashes before she could hide them from her assistant.

Bridget realized she touched a nerve because the girl eased out of the chair. Sarah eased as smoothly into the place the girl vacated. Focusing intently on the two prints, Sarah ran her finger down the exact spot Bridget had touched, the long chain with the beautiful silver, gold and black heart dangling low on her chest. Her throat closed, and she couldn't seem to breathe. Sarah took a deep, deep breath before she reminded Bridget.

"I couldn't find it, Bridget. Remember? I told you and Danny. That last morning...I couldn't find it. I was heartbroken. Reagan and I tore that place apart, but we never found it. All I had left were the earrings and memories of that necklace. It was there as we made love. It touched his skin in a thousand places...and I never found it."

Sobs finally shook Sarah, and she cried. She cried for the

morning she looked for that necklace but couldn't find it. She cried for every time a package came to her door, and she remembered Reagan and how much she loved him. She cried for her loneliness. Great overwhelming sobs of grief shook the woman. Sarah reached for the picture of Reagan and cradled it to her breasts. Finally, she bent double over the desk, laid the frame there, put her healed cheek on the cool glass covering his image, and she wept. Her misery was gentle, soft and pathetic.

"Cry, Doc. You've needed to cry for a long time now." Bridget hung a Do Not Disturb sign on the doorknob, stepped into the hall then closed and locked the door.

Sarah never said anything to Bridget about the incident, and the girl never alluded to it either. But both felt some good had come from the deluge of tears that afternoon.

———

Danny came in later that week with two magazines. One featured a photo layout by Reagan Conley. It showed the horrors of life in extreme northern Russia where the temperature killed, and many living there existed as their families had in the 1800s. It terrified Sarah to see the conditions under which he worked. The other magazine showed a series of action shots taken during a political coup in a South American country. Several shots showed men with firearms and high-powered rifles. Dead bodies, lying like discarded rag dolls, was featured on the next page. Sarah threw the magazine on her desk, suddenly sick at what she saw. Was Reagan all right? The letter with his latest package indicated he had to return to that horror. Did he make it out safely? She could only pray that his publicist would have contacted her if anything happened to him. She wouldn't feel better until his next picture and letter arrived.

November fifteenth came...and went. But Sarah expected that. The fifteenth was a Sunday, and Reagan always sent her package to the office. But Monday the sixteenth came and went. No package.

Sarah was distraught. After seeing the magazine articles, her imagination ran wild. Bridget and Danny didn't know what to say to her to make her feel better though Danny tried. "Maybe that storm delayed the mail, Doc."

Even the students in her classes were aware Dr. Malloy didn't get her package from Reagan Conley on time.

Everyone was tense in class the next day. Sarah constantly watched the classroom door. Bridget and Danny took turns manning the office. As soon as her package arrived, one of them would run it to her class. But the seventeenth passed without any sign of mail from Reagan.

Bridget and Danny couldn't look Sarah in the face the morning of November eighteenth. All kinds of wild things went through their imaginations.

"What if Mr. Conley has been hurt or worse? What if he's been killed, and Dr. Malloy doesn't know yet." Danny's theories got wilder and wilder.

"I don't think Dr. Malloy can live if anything happens to that man," Bridget whispered.

All three puttered around the office, but no one had their minds on the work they should be doing.

Danny and Sarah were looking over some papers around three o'clock that afternoon when they heard footsteps pounding up the staircase.

"Dr. Malloy! Dr. Malloy!" Bridget yelled at the top of her voice. They could hear her coming up the staircase before she even got into the second-floor hallway.

Sarah jumped out of her chair so quickly it rolled back

and bumped into Danny's desk. Fearing Bridget was hurt or something was critically wrong, Sarah ran from the room with Danny close on her heels. All three ran so fast they almost had a head-on collision right in the middle of the hall. Other staff members stuck their heads out of their doors to see what was going on. From the sounds of running and shouting, they could only assume the building was on fire.

"Dr. Malloy, Dr. Malloy, it came! It came!" Bridget screamed as she careened into Sarah. That was the only way Sarah figured she could safely stop the crazy woman running at her full-tilt. Bridget fell into Sarah's arms, both laughing and crying. Both women went down in a heap right in the middle of the hall.

Danny saw the pile but was running so fast and so close to Sarah that he couldn't have stopped if he had wanted to, so he went down across both women. All three sat up in a tangle of arms and legs, but Bridget had managed to keep the package wrapped in heavy brown paper held high so it was the only thing not crunched or tangled. They came up laughing, crying and whooping loud shouts of joy.

Bridget hugged Sarah. Sarah hugged her back, and both women hugged Danny. The staff took one look at the crazy trio, saw there was no national emergency, and returned to their offices after slamming their doors in noisy protest at being disturbed.

Sarah unscrambled her legs as Danny helped Bridget then Sarah stand.

"What happened, Bridget? Where'd the package come from? Why was it so late?" Sarah fired those questions at Bridget as the three headed to her office.

"I caught sight of the delivery man right outside. He remembered me from all the other times he's brought your package, so I convinced him to let me sign for it right there and save him the trip upstairs. I asked him why it was so late since it usually comes on the fifteenth like clockwork, and he reminded me that the Christmas mailing rush has already begun. Mail will be slow coming from now until after the New Year. That poor man must have thought I was a crazy woman because as soon as I got that package in my hand, I took off running and yelling at the top of my voice."

Sarah laughed until tears ran from her eyes. Danny slapped Bridget on the back and gave her a high five.

This time Sarah began jerking the wrapping paper off before she even entered her office. The mailing stamp indicated the package came from London. Well, at least Reagan was in civilization again. Or at least as much civilization as the Aussies will admit those in the U.K. have. Sarah chuckled but didn't take time to explain her thoughts to her two assistants.

Flinging the top cover off, Sarah stopped moving so suddenly that it seemed she froze in place. Here was a picture she hadn't anticipated. It was in black and white for one thing. And it was a close-up of her face. Her head lay on Reagan's shoulder right in that curve of his neck where he felt so warm and smelled so good...so masculine. She lay with her face turned away from him. She could only see the curve of Reagan's jaw, his ear, part of his hairline, the curve of his bare shoulder and the fingers of her hand where she clutched his warm neck.

Her face was the focus this time. Eyes closed; her face lay in anguish as a single tear rolled down from her eye across the top of her cheek. The look on her face and the pressure of her hand on his skin showed her heart. Showed what she was thinking in that moment of time. She didn't want to leave this man. She didn't want him to go. The photograph was poignant. The shades of black, white and gray gave the print more power, made the viewer more aware of the emotions going on there.

"Would you leave me alone for a while, guys?" Sarah asked.

"Sure, Doc."

Sarah heard the click of the door but nothing else.

"Oh, Reagan, when did you do this? Was it as you packed that steamer trunk? I remember you set up your little tripod and attached the camera to show me how the trip line worked so you could be in the picture or shot while standing away from the actual camera. I remember how you pulled me to you for a warm embrace when I looked unhappy. I didn't want to talk about you leaving. I didn't want you to go. But I never realized you actually took a picture that afternoon. Is that really me?" Sarah talked to the picture as if Reagan were right there with her.

The letter on the back echoed her sadness.

November 2015

My dearest Sarah,

How I long for this journey to be over. I have once again traveled around the globe, but still haven't found that destination as you said. I'm tired, Sarah. Seeing the world only makes me yearn for a corner of it to call my own. I never knew you cried that day, darling. You were so brave. It was only at the airport that I saw you break down. That made it so hard for me to leave you. I didn't want to go.

I want to hold you again, feel your heart beating under my palm, listen to you breathing close to my ear as you sleep, hear you laugh at my jokes. Only a little more to go. I'm so tired, Sarah. I miss you so much.

Love, Reagan

Her heart overflowed with love and tears. He missed her;

he must *love* her. He did sound tired. Even his writing wasn't as crisp as it usually was. When...when would he come home to her?

———

Dr. Malloy and her students entered the holiday season after Thanksgiving in high spirits. Snow would fall in swirling fury one day, then melt away the next. Days of weak winter sunshine never quite took the edge off the freezing temperature.

For some reason, Sarah felt renewed after Reagan's last letter. She still wrote a letter to him once a week. Each letter carried a message of love and yearning. Tender words slipped into her sentences. The man would have to be a blind fool not to know how she felt about him.

She looked forward to the holiday break because she intended to fly to New York and talk with Reagan's publicist. She wanted to find out where he was and join him. Excited over the prospect of seeing him soon, she sometimes sang aloud for no apparent reason.

Bridget and Danny even commented on her changed attitude. "What's up, Doc? You've been acting goofy ever since that last package showed up," Bridget asked as she straightened up her desk one late afternoon.

Hands on hips, a sneaky grin on her face, Sarah told them, "I'm going hunting over the holidays. I'm going to hunt down Reagan Conley."

"Way to go, Doc." Both of them gave her a high five.

"Remember that game, *Where in the World is Carmen San Diego*? Well, I'm doing that with a twist. *Where in the World is Reagan Conley.*"

"What are you going to do if you find him, Doc," Danny laughed even as he blushed. He had a vivid imagination.

Sarah gave them a seductive grin. "It's not a matter of *if*, my friend. It's *when*. And I'm not going to tell you what I'm going to do when I find him. Use your imaginations."

―――――

The last full day of fall semester classes was December third. That next day, Friday, would be a dead day for studying. Finals would begin the next Monday. Sarah met her last three classes that day, two in the morning and one at one o'clock. Both Danny and Bridget ran back and forth between her office and the classroom downstairs. Sarah had prepared some goodies for the kids in her class to enjoy, and her two T.A.s were in charge of keeping the food and drink coming.

Everyone cleared out after the morning class, and the three disappeared into Sarah's office. Even though she would see the two assistants sporadically during final exam time, Sarah wanted to give them their Christmas presents today at the lunch break.

Sarah gave each a present that he or she had mentioned wanting at one time or another.

Bridget got a journal. "Oh dang, Doc. That's awesome. I can..." She went off for a minute or two telling them how she planned to use it.

Danny got a backpack he'd admired for a long time but was too pricey for his limited budget. "Hey, Doc, you shouldn't have done this," he protested. "It's kind of expensive." Even as he said that, he was transferring things from his old bag to the new one. "Thanks, Doc," he said bashfully.

Then Bridget reached into her backpack and pulled out a small square box.

"This will remind you of some place you think a great deal of, Dr. M." she said, handing over the gift to Sarah.

"Oh Bridget, you know you didn't have to do this." Sarah

admonished. She knew how limited her budget was. Kissing Bridget on the cheek, she accepted the box, unwrapped it then opened it. Nestled in the dark blue velvet was a pin. It measured no more than two inches. A golden kangaroo bounced in front of a golden sun with rays spreading out in all directions.

"Oh, guys! A roo! Oz!" was all Sarah said, but her delight showed on her glowing face.

"I thought you'd like to wear it on your trench coat so when the weather around here really sucks sometimes, you can look at that and remember the sun...and the good times." Bridget blushed a little as she added that last part. To take the spotlight off her, she added as she watched Sarah rise and begin attaching the pin to the lapel of her coat, "Look what Danny did for you. That will really make you feel good...all year long!" She punched Danny on the arm as he stuck out a tube to Sarah.

"Come on, guys! You shouldn't have done all this! But," Sarah paused, "I love you for it!" She joined their laughter. Taking her seat once again, she carefully unwrapped the roll, expecting it to unravel into an explosion any minute. What finally emerged from the gaily-wrapped roll was a desk calendar. "You made this! Oh Danny, how cool!"

"I found all kinds of prints by Mr. Conley on the Internet, printed them out, and created a calendar. You can lay it on your desk, jot down memos on the numbers and enjoy the pictures on the upper half of the fold." Together they exclaimed over each one. The pictures were all familiar, of course, but it was so wonderful to have a copy of each one to enjoy as the months rolled by. Danny got a kiss and a hug for his Christmas contribution.

Putting their presents aside where they would be safe, the three returned to the classroom downstairs to prepare for the small party in the final class of the semester. As Sarah greeted her students when they entered the room, several kids complimented her on how pretty she looked that day which pleased her.

She tried to dress up just a little for them that day. Her short curly hair shone above a red sweater with a deep cowl draped neckline. Her skirt was red, green, gold and black plaid, and she finished the ensemble with a pair of glossy black knee-high boots. She felt very glamorous.

When one student complimented her, she thanked him then lovingly touched the heart-shaped earrings she always wore. If only she had found the matching necklace that last day, it would have gone perfectly with what she wore today. The momentary twinge of sadness disappeared in the face of so much high spirits abounding in her room. It was hard to be down for long in the midst of such youthful enthusiasm.

For the last time, she called roll and began the class. Of course, *class* quickly degenerated into a *party* with Bridget and Danny once again running back and forth getting supplies. Sarah stood talking to several kids when, from the corner of her eye, she caught Danny coming back into the room.

What's wrong with him? He's not carrying the bottle of pop I asked him to bring.

Before she could call him over, she saw that he was headed in her direction. He was carrying something, but it wasn't pop. Another package, but not the kind she was used to receiving, so she didn't think anything of it. Danny didn't stop right in front of her as she expected. He went around behind her and stopped, forcing Sarah to turn around and face him. The other students wandered away when they noticed Dr. Malloy had a rather put-out expression on her face.

"Danny," she whispered so as not to embarrass him, "what the heck are you doing? I sent you for some more drinks. What's this?" He had a rather peculiar expression on his face.

"Danny, are you all right?" she finally asked. He looked like a watch wound up too tightly, waiting to explode.

"This is for you, Doc." was all he could get out. He held the package out for her to see. Sarah frowned, looked at the thing that lay across his two hands then back at him.

"What is it?"

Danny shrugged. "Don't know. Better open it."

Sarah's hands were used to dealing with this kind of heavy brown wrapping paper, but twine held the paper together rather than the heavier cord she usually dealt with. "Hold it for me, will you, while I undo this twine."

"Be careful, Doc. There's something loose in there. I can hear it. Hope nothing's broken." Danny told her as she worked.

She nodded to show she heard him.

Sarah didn't get a funny feeling about the whole situation until she looked at the writing on the paper just before she pulled out the folded ends and prepared to remove the unwieldy mass of heavy brown paper. The writing was familiar, extremely familiar, but...there was no mailing stamp attached to the paper. She trembled just a bit. As she lifted the paper away from the content, she heard something slide over what sounded like glass. Frowning now, she moved quicker.

Everyone in the classroom had gone dead silent so the sliding noise across the glass sounded loud. Looking out of the corner of her eye, she could see all the students frozen in place, watching her.

Danny moved his hands enough to allow Sarah to uncover what he was holding. She whipped the paper off and froze, mouth open, eyes wide.

This wasn't *just* a print. This was a framed black and white portrait of Reagan and her. Two things, the tears that sprang immediately to her eyes and the object that lay entwined among the filigree edges of the picture frame obstructed her view of the picture.

The long chain of her necklace came loose to lay clutched in her grasp as she held it to her heart and sobbed. Where had it been? Where had he found it? Wiping away the tears, she reached for the photograph. Holding it in front of her, she studied it with a growing smile. Here at last was a picture of *both* of them...together...as they should be.

It was the first time Reagan had sent this kind of picture. She remembered...oh, she remembered that time when he asked her to come to the deck and pose with him. They looked out over the ocean...he to one side of her, pressed close to her side, his cheek resting against her temple. Her eyes wore a dreamy look. His arm curled around hers while the wind blew their hair and the opened front of that white shirt...the one she wore to bed every night. The necklace lie there, warm on her skin, as a symbol of their love. Oh, yes, she remembered.

"I was asked to deliver this personally, Doc," Danny said quietly.

"Oh, Reagan, I miss you so much." she whispered. In the tomb-like silence of her classroom that day, even she heard the whisper that came back to her.

"You were right, you know, Sarah. About that long winding road. The journey. The destination. That road led me back...to you. Standing here now gives me the greatest feeling of contentment and only enhances how right you are for me. I told myself I'd finish those few assignments that I couldn't get out of then have a long talk with you, but then I realized this won't be a long talk if you give me the answer I'm hoping for." He paused as if afraid to continue, worried that things might go amiss. "Marry me, Sarah? I can't live without you. I don't *want* to live without you." Reagan said it aloud at last. He stood bundled in a great coat, snowflakes still lying in his hair and looking so wonderful that it was hard for Sarah to breathe.

"Oh, Reagan, yes, a million times. Sharon once asked me if I'd be okay, and I said I'd be fine. Then I met you, and now I'm so fine I could just bust. Yes, yes, yes, my darling."

If the staff at Princeton thought Dr. Malloy's class loud at times, it was nothing to what erupted that day as Sarah Malloy flew across her classroom and threw herself into the arms of the only man she would ever love. Thunderous claps, stomping and whistles rolled down the halls and surrounded the two as they kissed, not for the first time, but not for the last times in what would be a long lifetime together.

Not the end but the beginning of a long winding road —together.

———

Don't miss out on your next favorite book!

Join the Satin Romance mailing list
www.satinromance.com/mail.html

THANK YOU FOR READING

Did you enjoy this book?

We invite you to leave a review at the website of your choice, such as Goodreads, Amazon, Barnes & Noble, etc.

————

DID YOU KNOW THAT LEAVING A REVIEW...

- Helps other readers find books they may enjoy.
- Gives you a chance to let your voice be heard.
- Gives authors recognition for their hard work.
- Doesn't have to be long. A sentence or two about why you liked the book will do.

About the Author

A varied life for me—student, teacher, wife, mom, writer, editor, quilter and an adventurer when possible. My goal? Do something outrageous every day. Doesn't always happen, but I try.

Jane also writes young adult fiction under the name Jane Grace. Find her books at our YA imprint, Fire and Ice Young Adult Books.

www.romances-by-janie.com
www.JaneGracePresents.com

Read my blogs:
lifesreruns.com
samewords-newways.com

Also by Jane R. Carver

With Melange Books
Forever Changed

The Gilpin Girls

With Satin Romance
Return With Honor

The Answer Key

A Long Winding Road

Anthologies
Western Ways, *Winning the Ranger's Heart*

———

Young Adult Novels as Jane Grace
with Fire & Ice Young Adult Books
Until I'm Safe

Ghosts In My Souls